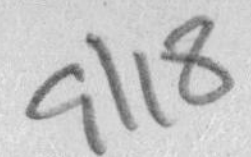

How had Juliet never really noticed how ripped Evan was?

His black T-shirt didn't do much to hide the muscles of his biceps, pecs or abs. Thank God.

Evan turned to the fridge for a couple of water bottles.

"You want?" Evan held up a bottle, his dimple showing with his smile.

Looking at him, Juliet realized she did indeed want.

Evan. Right now. Tonight.

She knew he wanted her, too. This wasn't just an undercover op for Evan. *She* wasn't just an undercover op for Evan.

This time she didn't plan to take no for an answer. She had let the attack steal too many months of her life. She didn't plan to let it have even one more day. She wanted Evan and she knew he wanted her.

What was that saying? Leap and the net will appear.

Juliet leaped.

She slid her own jacket off and walked over to him. "Yeah, I want."

UNTRACEABLE

JANIE CROUCH

To my Stephanie: it never ceases to amaze me that you call me your friend. You are a tireless source of support, inspiration and encouragement not just to me but to so many others. Here's some #nofilter for you: you are a treasure, a beauty, and someone who radiates God's love and kindness in everything you do. I adore you.

Recycling programs for this product may not exist in your area.

ISBN-13: 978-0-373-69840-0

Untraceable

This edition published by arrangement with Harlequin Books S.A.

For questions and comments about the quality of this book, please contact us at CustomerService@Harlequin.com.

Printed in U.S.A.

Janie Crouch has loved to read romance her whole life. She cut her teeth on Harlequin Romance novels as a preteen, then moved on to a passion for romantic suspense as an adult. Janie lives with her husband and four children overseas. Janie enjoys traveling, long-distance running, movie-watching, knitting and adventure/obstacle racing. You can find out more about her at janiecrouch.com.

Books by Janie Crouch

Omega Sector series

Infiltration
Countermeasures
Untraceable

HARLEQUIN INTRIGUE

Primal Instinct

CAST OF CHARACTERS

Juliet Branson—Once an active undercover agent for Omega Sector before she was attacked and left for dead. Now, unable to get past that event, she works as a handler/analyst for Omega.

Evan Karcz—Juliet's ex-partner and current Omega agent. Overwhelmed with guilt for being unable to protect Juliet when she was an agent, he will do anything to protect her now.

Dennis Burgamy—Juliet and Evan's boss at Omega Sector. Seems to care more about his own reputation than the safety of his agents.

Vince Cady—Crime boss with his fingers into almost every piece of ugliness imaginable: weapons, technology, blackmail, just to name a few.

Christopher Cady—Vince Cady's son. Being groomed to take on the family business, but has a sinister agenda of his own.

Heath Morel—Known associate of both Vince Cady and the attackers from Juliet's past. Seems to have information about Juliet that couldn't possibly be available to anyone else.

Cameron Branson—Juliet's brother and Omega operative, currently on active recovery due to wounds from a mission gone wrong.

Dylan Branson—Juliet's oldest brother. Former Omega operative and current pilot.

Sawyer Branson—Juliet's youngest and most laid-back brother. Omega operative, also on active recovery because of wounds received during an Omega mission.

Megan Fuller—Sawyer's fiancée and a computer genius.

Chapter One

Evan Karcz woke up the same way he had almost every day for the past year and a half: with Juliet Branson's terrified sobs echoing through his dreams.

Evan didn't jump out of bed and grab his Glock as he had in the early days. Nor did he have to rush to the bathroom before he lost the contents of his stomach.

Now he just breathed in and out slowly, calming his pounding heart, staring up at the ceiling. He threw the covers off his body in an effort to chill down, even though it was early spring and the temperatures were still cool here in southern Maryland, near Washington, DC. Evan wiped with his arm the small amount of sweat that beaded on his forehead.

He didn't lie there long. It was early, not even close to 5:00 a.m., but the possibility of going back to sleep was pretty much nonexistent. He might as well get up and start moving. He slipped on shorts and sweats and packed a gym bag with clothes for the rest of his day.

He'd head in to Omega Sector Headquarters and get in a workout before work officially started. *Exercise in order to exorcise*, Evan thought, and smiled grimly. Anything would be better than staying in that big bed by himself with nothing surrounding him but his own guilt.

Given the day ahead and all it had in store, he shouldn't

be surprised that the dream had resurfaced with such vividness. Today he'd be unable to avoid seeing the subject of his troubled dreams—his ex-partner, Juliet Branson. Although *avoid* wasn't really accurate. Evan never tried to avoid seeing Juliet; the opposite, in fact. He'd been trying to talk to her for eighteen months, with no real success. Today, Juliet would be unable to avoid seeing *him*.

Evan drove to Omega Headquarters, thankful that the early hour at least helped shorten the notoriously ugly commute. He pulled into the secure parking garage of the nondescript building that housed Omega Sector—a covert interagency task force made up of the best personnel the country had to offer. Evan had worked here for eight years, ever since his recruitment out of the FBI when he was twenty-seven.

The heaviness from this morning's dream lingered as he walked through the doors of Omega's main building. Strange how these halls had once thrilled him, how he had loved everything about his job as an undercover agent. But since Juliet's…incident he couldn't seem to find the same passion he'd once had for the work.

Passionate or not, he was going back under. And he wasn't looking forward to the team meeting that would take place later today, when Juliet would learn the details of the assignment. Evan rubbed a hand over his face. He knew Bob Sinclair, his undercover persona, was a name Juliet would never want to hear again. Nobody blamed her for that.

Omega Headquarters stood largely empty at this hour except for the security personnel. Evan passed through the extensive checks to confirm his identity, then jogged down the stairs into the large gym area. State-of-the-art workout equipment stood side by side with old-school metal weights, a fitting metaphor for Omega: the best blend of new and old techniques, working in unison. There were also rooms for sparring, for yoga, and a full-size track for running. Evan left his gym bag in the locker room and walked into the main workout area.

Sparring definitely topped the agenda for this morning. Evan decided he might as well take his aggression out on the almost-human plastic dummies and leather punching bags, since the individuals he really wanted to take his aggression out on were well beyond his reach.

He grabbed a pair of gloves meant to save his knuckles from the worst of the damage, and was reaching for the doorknob of the sparring room when he heard noises from someone already in there. Who the hell would be up and going at this hour?

Evan let the door shut and walked around the corner so he could see through the small window of the room. Juliet Branson…

Evidently he hadn't been the only one with nightmares this morning.

Evan couldn't help but watch, enthralled, as she danced among the targets with grace and precision. The black tank and tight workout pants she wore gave her the freedom to move as she wanted, stopping sometimes midair and pivoting in a different direction. Her five-foot-four-inch frame was average in height—at six-one Evan was a full head taller than her—but the way she fought belied her smaller stature, the litheness of her muscles evident. Her long blond hair was pulled tightly back in a ponytail, so as not to impede her actions.

The power behind her kicks and punches was impressive. Had these dummies been live people, each would've fallen to the ground, gasping for air. She showed them, and herself, no mercy. Rapid-fire strikes. Over and over, at a punishing speed and rhythm. Sweat dripped and flew with each of her assaults. You'd never be able to tell she'd been out of the field for the past eighteen months.

Evan watched from the shadows of the hallway, where she wouldn't be able to see him. As a trained operative, he recognized and appreciated Juliet's talent in close-quarter fighting like this, although admittedly, fighting dummy targets was completely different than fighting a real opponent.

She attacked the dummies as if she were warding off a demon army from hell. Evan's arms hung at his sides and his shoulders slumped. Fighting demons was probably an apt description for her actions.

He wished he could fight them for her. Or at least with her, but Juliet had no interest in being anywhere near him. Not that he could blame her. A partner was supposed to have your back, to protect you, even in dire circumstances. Evan had failed her in the worst possible way. And Juliet had paid a horrible price for his failure.

He turned and walked the other way, leaving her to her battle. Entering the room would just cause her to tense up and rapidly vacate, anyway. But not before fear and distrust suffused her features when the door first opened. It wasn't just him she distrusted, Evan knew, but he hated the look, anyway.

Plus, he'd be seeing it soon enough, later today in the conference room, when he mentioned Bob Sinclair.

Evan headed up the stairs to the indoor track. It seemed as if he would be trying to outrun his own demons today rather than fighting them. But no matter how fast he ran, he knew they'd still be there when he finished.

JULIET SWUNG HER LEG around in a powerful round-house kick, hitting the target one last time. She took satisfaction in how hard the dummy fell to the ground before its weighted bottom slowly brought it back to a vertical position.

Yeah, she could take down a target dummy like a champ. Too bad that didn't really do anybody much good. In a fight with a real person these days, she was damn near useless.

Of course, Juliet wasn't an active agent anymore, so it wasn't as if she was going to use her hand-to-hand fighting skills anytime soon. But it would be nice to know she'd have them if she needed them, rather than freezing up or cowering in a corner if a real person came at her.

Juliet backhanded the dummy again for good measure.

She grabbed a towel and mopped up her sweat from the past hour of pounding everything in sight. It was now just before 5:00 a.m., and there'd be other people around soon, if not already. Dedicated Omega workers—agents and otherwise—would come in to get a good workout before going upstairs to their jobs.

Juliet would like to think that was what she was doing, too. That she was here at Omega HQ sometimes eighteen or twenty hours a day because of her dedication to an important job and stellar organization. That she worked long hours because she wanted to do her part in keeping her country safe from criminals and terrorists.

Not because of the fear that seemed to pour over her like some sort of suffocating ooze every time she left this place.

It was so much easier to stay here at Omega than to go home alone to her house. Juliet felt safe here, even when she was by herself. There was no chance someone was going to throw a sack over her head and drag her out of a sound sleep in the middle of the night. Of course, there was very little chance that would happen at her home, but Juliet couldn't quite seem to convince her mind of that as she lay awake at night, terrified, remembering. So she stayed here at Omega as much as possible.

It had been eighteen months since her attack. Things should be getting better, not worse. But that wasn't the case.

She glanced down at her phone, which had begun vibrating in her hand as she walked toward the locker room. Her stomach rolled when she saw the screen.

A new email. Not for Juliet Branson, but for Lisa Sinclair, an undercover role Juliet had played in her last mission as an active operative. The one where she'd lost nearly everything.

Sweetheart, I've been thinking about you all night. Soon we'll be together, just the two of us. Sooner than you think.

As usual, no signature or notification of who'd sent it. Juliet leaned against the wall for support and brought her hand up to her suddenly aching head. This email was benign compared to the graphic nature of some of the others. She closed her eyes briefly, pushing those thoughts away. She couldn't let this overwhelm her, not today.

But she knew she'd be thinking about the message all day. And the fact that the emails were starting to come more frequently and become more personal.

Juliet had given the emails to Omega tech support, of course, but they hadn't been able to provide any insight about where or from whom they were coming. Never the same IP address—it seemed to bounce around all over the world.

And she couldn't bring herself to tell anyone about how much the emails upset her. She knew there were people here who cared about her. Two of her three brothers worked at Omega, for goodness' sake; she saw them almost every day. But they were the last people she wanted to talk to about this. Being the only daughter in the family, Juliet had always been surrounded by overprotective, alpha-male testosterone.

Talking to her brothers about residual issues from her attack and rape? Um, no. Not in this lifetime.

Nor did she want to talk to them about creepy emails. Her siblings had work to do, *real* cases to worry about.

"Hey, Jules, you okay?"

Juliet pushed herself away from the wall at the sound of Evan Karcz's voice. He, like her brothers, always called her Jules. She mashed the button to delete the email notification and turn her phone screen black. She didn't want to have to explain it to Evan.

"Um, yeah, I'm fine. Just going in to clean up after my workout. You're here early."

"I was about to run, but I forgot my headphones and was coming back to grab them. You sure you're okay? You look a little pale. And you must have been sparring because you have something in your—"

Evan moved toward her, hand upraised, and before Juliet could stop herself she took a step back, flinching. He froze, then dropped his arm to his side, shoulders drooping.

"Evan, I'm sorry—"

"No, it's okay. Um, you just have some lint or something in your hair." He backed up another step. "I'll see you." He turned and walked off, away from the locker room. So much for getting headphones.

Juliet wanted to hit something, even though she'd just spent over an hour doing just that. She hadn't meant to flinch, especially not from Evan; she'd just been in a particularly vulnerable state of mind because of that email. It didn't take a genius to figure out her reaction had hurt him.

She and Evan had worked together for years. She'd

known him most of her life. He was her brothers' best friend. Hell, he was one of *her* best friends—more, if she was honest. Or had potentially been more. It seemed so long ago that she and Evan used to flirt with each other, secure in the knowledge of *someday*.

But someday never came.

Now whenever she thought of Evan all Juliet could recall was that moment when he'd found her. Of how he'd covered her broken, mostly naked body with his own clothes, actually crying as he had radioed in for an ambulance.

Juliet knew it was unfair to keep Evan frozen in that moment. To keep *herself* frozen there. But she couldn't seem to do anything about it.

So she'd basically avoided him for the past year and a half.

Which hadn't been too difficult, considering her cowardly choice to leave active work and stick herself behind a desk instead. Part handler, part analyst, part strategist. A little too good to be any of them, but not fit to be back out in the field. Juliet couldn't see a time when she would ever be ready for agent work again.

Her job might not be thrilling, but it was safe. And safe was the most important thing to her right now. Although she wished those job changes hadn't hurt Evan.

Juliet made her way to the locker room, showering and changing into her work clothes of black pants and a matching black blazer over a white blouse. The jacket was specially fitted to hold her shoulder holster and firearm. Although Juliet wasn't an agent and wasn't required to be armed at all times, she was rarely without her Glock 9 mm.

Normally she wouldn't be dressed this way. Unlike the FBI, with their daily suits and loafers, Omega tended to be a more casually dressed workforce. But today Juliet had an important operational-specifications meeting. Her boss, Dennis Burgamy, would be there, which made her a little uneasy. Burgamy did not tend to dirty his hands with the day-to-day planning of undercover operations. Thus her more professional suit: armor for battle.

Something was up; she knew it. Juliet was going to need as much armor as she could get.

Chapter Two

Juliet already sat in the conference room between her brothers Cameron and Sawyer, chatting with both, when Evan arrived at the meeting. He wasn't surprised to find the two men flanking Juliet. If Cameron and Sawyer had their way, she'd be wrapped in cotton wool and hidden away somewhere.

The Branson men were brothers to Evan in every way but blood. He'd known them most of his life—Sawyer, Cameron, and their older brother, Dylan, who no longer worked at Omega—and would do anything for any of them. But their overprotectiveness when it came to Juliet frustrated Evan.

Juliet had strength none of the Branson family wanted to admit, including herself. Right now it lay hidden under layers of fear and regret. But the strength resided inside her. He'd seen it multiple times during their tenure as partners in the field. He wished Juliet would trust him to help her find that strength again, but he couldn't force it to happen. Could only wait and hope.

Evan deliberately took the seat directly across from Juliet. She nodded at him and gave him a polite smile before looking away. He decided to engage her brothers instead.

"What's up, Tweedledum and Tweedledummer?"

Neither brother was up to his normal speed. Both were

recovering from gunshot wounds received in action over the past few months, Cameron from an undercover operation gone wrong, and Sawyer from an attempt to fix that. They would recover fully, but were manning desks until they were cleared for field duty.

Not that either seemed to mind desk duty right now. It gave them each more time to spend at home with the loves-of-their-lives, also recently acquired in the cases. Having met Cameron's Sophia and Sawyer's Megan, Evan wholeheartedly supported his friends wanting to stick close to home.

"Watch it there, shorty. I can still kick your butt even with my arm in this sling," Sawyer told him. The "shorty" barb had been around since they were all teenagers and Evan had been the last to hit his growth spurt, so he'd been a head shorter than the Branson boys for a time. Even though they now were all around the same height—each over six feet— Evan still got called shorty from time to time. But it brought the slightest of smiles to Juliet's lips, so he let it slide.

"Yeah, I'd hate to put your other arm in a sling," Evan retorted.

"Why are we having a big powwow with Burgamy?" Cameron cut in, referring to their boss, Dennis Burgamy. "Since when does he sit in on normal op-specification meetings?"

"I was wondering the same thing myself." Juliet glanced briefly at Evan before turning away.

Evan knew he had to tell her about him going back undercover as Sinclair. He didn't want her to hear it for the first time in the middle of the meeting.

"I don't know why Burgamy wants to be in the meeting exactly," Evan said. "But you guys should know that I'm going back under as Bob Sinclair."

Cameron muttered a curse. Sawyer didn't say anything. He'd already been aware that the Sinclair persona had been resurrected a few weeks ago. Evan had posed as Bob Sinclair to help Sawyer out in a case.

The color washed out of Juliet's face and she stood, her chair rolling back from the table forcefully. All three men stood, as well.

"Excuse me," she murmured.

"Jules—" Sawyer reached for her, but stopped when she flinched away.

"No, I'm all right. I'll be back in a minute."

Evan watched as she all but fled from the room. He gave a heavy sigh and sat back down.

"Should one of us go after her?" Cameron asked.

"No, let her go," Evan said. "She just needs to pull herself together."

Sawyer and Cameron looked as though they might argue, but decided against it. Evan knew he was right. Juliet would not want any of them coming after her, crowding her space. She'd be back when she was ready, which would probably be sooner than either of her overprotective brothers suspected.

Evan hated Juliet hearing about the Bob Sinclair situation this way, but knew it would have upset her no matter when or how she heard about it. There was no way around that.

Dennis Burgamy, head of operations at Omega, entered the room along with his assistant, Chantelle DiMuzio, who looked harried. Of course, poor Chantelle always looked harried. Anybody who worked that closely with their boss day in and day out couldn't help it.

Burgamy took the seat at the head of the table, glanced around, and turned to Evan. "Where's Juliet?"

"She had to step out. She'll be back soon."

Burgamy, dressed impeccably in a dark suit, sighed impatiently. Everyone knew there was no love lost between him and the Branson family. Each side tolerated the other, but only barely. Usually Burgamy didn't have much problem with Juliet, however. Why had he even asked about her?

"Well, I don't have much spare time, so we'll need to start without her," Burgamy barked.

"Okay, to get everyone up to speed," Evan began, trying to stall to give Juliet time to return. "In the midst of Sawyer's operation last month with Dr. Megan Fuller and DS-13, we weren't sure if the Ghost Shell hardware system was going to be sold on the black market. Or if we would have the means of stopping it if it was sold."

"A disaster on all counts," Burgamy said.

Everyone nodded. Evan continued. "We were in a time crunch so I put feelers out on the street using some past covers, in case I needed to infiltrate any black market weapons groups."

Evan looked over at Sawyer. "Fortunately, Sawyer was able to acquire Ghost Shell and arrest or eliminate most of DS-13, whom we are considering permanently disbanded."

Sawyer raised an eyebrow. That wasn't exactly how the whole thing had gone down, but whatever. Close enough.

Evan looked up, his attention caught by Juliet coming back through the door.

"Sorry," she murmured to Burgamy, before taking her seat between her brothers once again.

Her features were still a little pinched, but she seemed otherwise well composed. As Evan knew, she was stronger than she thought.

"I was just explaining the situation with Sawyer and DS-13 last month," he said to her. "You already know all of that."

Juliet nodded. She did know it. As a matter of fact, she was the reason Sawyer and his fiancé, Megan Fuller, had gotten out alive at all.

"In the midst of that operation, one of my feelers got a lot of response—Bob Sinclair." Juliet flinched as Evan said it, but he continued. "First, it was DS-13 who expressed interest, but since then someone from Vince Cady's group has made contact."

That got everyone's attention. Vince Cady was a crime boss with his fingers in almost every piece of ugliness you could find: weapons, technology, blackmail. On the surface he looked clean, and did a good job of covering his tracks. Omega had never found anything that could be used to indict Cady, but they knew he was dirty. And even more, he was key to a number of larger groups and sellers. If Omega could get dirt on Cady, they could take down a lot of other bad guys.

Vince Cady was known as a grade-A bastard. Smooth, but with a cruel edge. And very, *very* smart. Which was why he'd never been arrested.

Cady initiating contact with Bob Sinclair provided a huge break for Omega. Having an undercover foothold in his group would be measurable progress, bringing Omega much closer to taking Cady and his network down.

"That's excellent," Cameron said. "It gives Bob Sinclair instant credibility. Cady came to you, not the other way around."

Evan nodded. "Yes, I plan to use that fact to my advantage as much as possible."

"Did he contact you for a specific buy?" Burgamy asked.

Juliet spoke up. "Our most recent intel about Cady suggests that he may have acquired some surface-to-air missiles to sell on the black market. That would be a perfect fit for Bob Sinclair."

Juliet's voice wavered only the slightest bit when she said it.

Evan nodded in encouragement. "I agree," he told the group. "Bob and Lisa Sinclair's reputation is as entrepreneurs. They..." Evan looked over and saw Juliet's pinched features as well as Sawyer and Cameron's thunderous looks, so changed his pronoun choice. "Bob, I mean, is known as a jack-of-all-trades, dabbling in weapons, pharmaceutical drugs, technology, information. He's the type of guy who can help Vince Cady out, so I'm not surprised by the contact."

"Okay, good," Burgamy said. Chantelle, sitting next to him, kept clicking away, taking notes on her tablet the entire time. "What's the timetable for this op?"

Evan still didn't know why Burgamy was even here. Yes, Cady was a pretty big fish and infiltrating his group would be a huge coup, but why the boss would sit in on an early planning meeting like this was beyond Evan.

"I have a meeting scheduled with Cady tomorrow in Baltimore, his base of operation. Since Bob Sinclair is an old cover, I'm just going to pull and use all the old info, IDs, etc. Prep is relatively minimal. I can go under immediately, depending on how the meeting with Cady goes."

"Eighteen months absence isn't going to be a problem?" Burgamy asked.

"Yeah, I'm sure it will come up. I'll make certain I have something to say." Evan didn't know what that would be yet. The truth wasn't an option, and the whole situation with Lisa Sinclair was quite complicated. Evan would have multiple answers rehearsed, depending on exactly what questions were asked, how they were asked, and the climate of the conversation.

That's what a good undercover agent did: constantly took stock of the situation and adapted.

"And what about Lisa Sinclair, Bob's 'wife'?" Burgamy asked.

And there it was, the announcement of the elephant in the room. Evan didn't look over at Juliet to see her reaction. She didn't need anyone gawking at her.

"What about her?" Evan responded, keeping his tone neutral.

"Bob and Lisa Sinclair were a couple. A tight couple." Burgamy leaned more of his weight on his arms, which were folded on the conference table. "The cover worked so well because the criminal groups you infiltrated bought into the whole Bonnie and Clyde, can't-live-without-each-other vibe the two of you gave off."

Evan didn't want to admit it, but Burgamy was right. Going in without Juliet would make this mission more difficult. But the alternative wasn't an option, so Evan wasn't even entertaining it as such. He glanced briefly over at Juliet, who was looking intently down at her notes.

"I'll make it work, as Bob Sinclair alone. I've certainly done my share of undercover work with no partner." Evan could see the Branson brothers nodding, backing him up. Cameron in particular knew about long-term solo undercover work, having recently come off a life-changing operation himself.

But Burgamy wasn't willing to let it go. "Isn't Cady going to wonder about Lisa? Her absence will certainly make suspicions higher, perhaps even jeopardize the entire mission."

Evan sat up straighter in his chair, then leaned toward Burgamy. He could see Juliet's brothers mirroring his actions, tension evident. Evan didn't like where this was going.

"I'm a trained, experienced operative, Burgamy. I'll handle it."

The boss's smile didn't reach his eyes. "I have every confidence in your abilities, Karcz. But the facts are the facts."

Burgamy leaned back in the chair in a relaxed pose that belied the words he'd said. Suddenly the entire meeting became clear to Evan, the purpose of Burgamy's attendance and his endgame. And Evan had played right into his hands. He knew what Burgamy was going to say before his boss even said it, but there was nothing he could do.

Burgamy turned to Juliet. "Juliet needs to go back undercover as Lisa Sinclair to ensure the success of this operation."

Chapter Three

Juliet heard the words that came out of Burgamy's mouth as if from far away. She searched for a response inside herself—knew she should have some sort of explosive negative comment—but could find only silence.

She couldn't go back undercover as Lisa Sinclair. She wasn't ready. It would be a disaster.

It ended up she didn't have to give an answer, anyway. Her brothers took care of the explosive negative comments for her.

"There's no way in hell, Burgamy," Sawyer, her normally laid-back younger brother, said grimly.

The expletive that came from Cameron should've had her smacking his arm or at least telling him to chill out. But Juliet still could find only silence.

Both brothers stood, now in an open argument with Burgamy, listing the reasons Juliet couldn't go back undercover as Lisa Sinclair. She wasn't ready, Burgamy couldn't force her, she hadn't had the needed prep time… Juliet just tuned them out as they continued.

She knew her weaknesses, knew she was a coward. She didn't need to listen to an active discussion of those facts.

Juliet looked up from her folded hands to find Evan staring at her across the table.

She could find no pity in his gaze. Nor disappointment. He actually shrugged and rolled his eyes, gesturing casually with his hand to all the chaos. As if the yelling currently reverberating through the conference room came from preschoolers throwing temper tantrums about sharing their favorite toys, rather than Juliet's boss asking her to do something that would probably get both her and Evan killed.

How could Evan take it so lightly?

Juliet rubbed a hand over her face. There was no point in letting her brothers get in trouble with Burgamy—*again*—over this. The choice belonged to her and she already knew her answer.

She stood up, but didn't try to yell over her brothers, just waited for them to realize she had something to say. Over the years she had perfected that practice.

Eventually everyone grew silent and looked at her.

"No. I won't do it." Juliet said it plainly, not raising her voice in any way.

"Juliet," Burgamy began in his nasally tone, "it's evident that the mission has a greater chance for success if you are part of it."

"I disagree," she said.

Burgamy had no intention of giving up so easily. "But Vince Cady and his people will be expecting you to be with Evan. Bob and Lisa Sinclair are a known couple."

Juliet held up a hand to silence her boss. "My initial presence might be an asset, I concur. But for any longer term I would just be a liability. Evan can't babysit me and successfully complete the mission."

Now it was Evan who spoke up. "Jules—"

She turned to him, could see the anguish in his eyes.

"No, Evan. I'm not of any use to anybody in the field right now. Trust me."

Burgamy was determined to continue his argument. "But—"

Juliet decided to put a stop to it right now and save them all the trouble. "Respectfully, Burgamy, I'm not an agent anymore. You can't force me to do this. So let's not pretend like you can, okay? I'm not going back in the field as Lisa Sinclair." She turned to Evan. "I won't risk your life that way."

Burgamy wisely didn't say anything further. He knew Juliet's words were true. After what had happened to her the last time, no one at Omega would ever try to force her into an undercover assignment. If she ever went under again, it would be her own choice.

Juliet didn't see that happening anytime soon, say, for the next twenty years.

She noticed both her brothers sitting down, evidently accepting the battle was over. Which it was.

"I'll help Evan in any way I can," Juliet said. "I'm willing to be the support team leader, so I can use my experience to assist him."

She spoke to Burgamy as she said it, but saw Evan's surprised look out of the corner of her eye. It was no wonder; for the year that she'd been working as a handler, she'd never volunteered to oversee any of his cases. She'd done some strategy and analysis support for him, but never anything that would keep them in daily contact.

Working as Evan's handler would definitely bring the two of them in regular contact. She'd just have to deal with that. Juliet frowned and rubbed the back of her neck. Maybe she was too much of a coward to go back out in the field, but she could at least help him from the safety of Omega Headquarters. She knew staff support wasn't what Evan really needed from her. Plenty of people were qualified to act as his handler, her two wounded brothers being prime examples. What Evan needed from her was in the field.

Disgust with herself pitted her stomach.

Burgamy, having evidently failed in his purpose for being at the meeting, excused himself and left. His assistant trailed after him. With them gone, some of the tension left the room, and quiet conversations started up.

Juliet looked over at Evan's handsome face as he spoke to Sawyer about Vince Cady. Evan's brown hair, cut short and stylishly, and his beautiful hazel eyes, were in sharp contrast to her brother's darker looks. A small scar marred Evan's cheek, hardly a centimeter from his left eye. He'd gotten it during a case they'd worked on together, three years ago.

Evan had fought the bodyguard of a drug lord they'd been investigating. The huge, muscular guard, having found out the two of them were law enforcement, had decided Evan needed only one eye. The thug would've been successful in that little venture if Juliet hadn't helped wrestle the knife away.

She still smiled a little whenever she thought of that case. Evan had joked a few weeks later, at a Branson family barbecue, that the scar was okay because it finally made him as ugly as her brothers. As if any of them could be called ugly.

It had been a long time since Juliet had been to one of her family's barbecues. She wondered if Evan still went, even without her there for the past year and a half. Probably. Her brothers were his best friends.

The next couple hours were spent discussing details of the case. Evan would meet Vince Cady two days from now, at a place yet to be determined by Cady in Baltimore, which was less than an hour away from DC. There were a lot of unknowns in the case, things Evan would have to figure out on the fly, not unusual in undercover work.

The primary objective of the case wasn't the arrest of Vince Cady. Leaving him in play in order to get information on his other contacts and pipelines took precedence. So, although they'd all like to see him behind bars as soon as possible, that wouldn't happen immediately. Instead, recovery of the surface-to-air missiles—the SAMs—that Cady wanted to sell would be the primary objective. Omega couldn't allow them to be sold to enemies of the United States.

And Evan would be the sole person stopping that from happening.

Juliet ignored the tiny voice inside her that said this mission was too much for one person, even someone as capable as Evan, to handle on his own. Evan would be just fine. And he wouldn't be alone; he'd have plenty of support from the team here at Omega.

Juliet pretended that was enough. Because what else could she do?

Eventually, the meeting wound down as they worked out as many details as they could. The team trickled out one by one, each sure of his or her own assignments. Sawyer and Cameron both hugged her as they left to go back to their own cases, wishing Evan luck, offering their support whenever it was needed.

Juliet grabbed her own items, preparing to go to her office. She had a lot to do before Evan's meeting with Vince Cady.

"Can I walk with you?" Evan asked her.

"Sure." They stepped out of the conference room together and down the hall. It had been a long time since

Juliet had talked to Evan, just the two of them. It felt… weird. But not as awkward as she would've expected.

"I just wanted to let you know I had no idea Burgamy was going to say all that junk," Evan told her. Juliet noticed he was careful to keep a distance from her and not touch or crowd her in any way as they were walking. "I mean, I knew I would be resuming the role of Bob Sinclair, but I didn't think Burgamy would suggest you go back under as Lisa."

Juliet swallowed and tried to make light of it. "You know Burgamy, always willing to do whatever it takes to get the job done."

"More like, always willing to do whatever it takes to get credit and recognition from his superior officers."

Juliet nodded. Burgamy definitely had his eye on a position much higher than the one he currently held.

They arrived at Juliet's office, one of the few perks of working as an analyst was having an office rather than just a desk like active operatives, and she entered. She thought Evan would say his goodbyes and head out, but he followed her in. She placed the case files on her desk and turned to him.

"You look very nice today," Evan said, leaning against the wall near the door. "Professional."

Compared to the jeans and sweater she normally wore, that was probably true. "Thanks." Juliet half smiled. "I wanted to put in an effort, since Burgamy was attending the meeting. Although if I had known why, I wouldn't have bothered."

Evan grimaced. "I don't blame you."

"So you feel ready to take on Bob Sinclair again?" As soon as Juliet uttered the words she wished she could take them back. She didn't want to talk about Evan's feelings regarding Sinclair any more than she would want to talk about hers if she was resuming the role of Lisa.

"Yeah, sure." Evan shrugged. "Can't miss an opportunity like this with someone like Vince Cady."

"Good." Juliet didn't know what else to say.

"Look, Jules..." Evan took a step from the wall. "I just wanted you to know, *make sure* you know, that nobody, even Burgamy, expects you to resume Lisa Sinclair. Burgamy wanted to try, had to try just in case, but he didn't really expect you to do it."

Juliet appreciated the sentiment from Evan, although she wasn't sure if he was correct.

"I know your brothers want to protect you, which is why they were so adamant in there this morning," he continued. "They love you and don't want anything bad to happen to you again."

"Thanks, Evan." Juliet was tentative, not sure what his point was.

"And, of course, I *never...*" Evan ran his hands through his hair, seeming to need a moment to gather himself. "I never want you to go through anything like that again."

Anguish was evident in his face. Juliet hurt for him. Ironic, since he was hurting for her.

"Evan—"

"But I want you to know something, Jules," he added. "Although I would never try to talk you into going undercover against your will, you are capable of much more than you give yourself credit for. You can be a good agent again, if you decide to be."

He said it with so much conviction that, somewhere deep inside, Juliet wished it were true.

Thought maybe, just for a second, that it could be.

But then she thought of this morning, how she'd gotten another of those stupid emails and had let it completely derail her *again*. How she arrived every day at Omega Headquarters at 4:00 a.m. because she was too scared to stay in her own house alone. She thought of the overwhelming panic that occurred whenever someone, however innocently, touched her from behind. She thought of all the ways she had screwed up the last mission, and the price she had paid for it.

And she thought of Evan and how *he* would be the one to suffer, or worse, if she went back out in the field and couldn't perform her duties.

Evan wanted to support her, and Juliet appreciated his kind words, but he didn't know all the facts. No matter what he said, Juliet would never again be a good agent.

"I'm sorry I'm sending you out there alone, Evan. I know it's a sucky thing to do."

"No." He shook his head. "This isn't about me or Bob Sinclair or this case at all. I'll be fine. The case will be fine. I just wanted you to know that I think—that I *know*—you can do it. When you're ready."

Chapter Four

Evan watched as Juliet shuffled some papers, made a flimsy excuse about needing to be somewhere, and all but fled out the door. She didn't make eye contact with him the entire time. Of course, she didn't have to, for him to know what she was thinking.

That there was no way she'd ever be a good agent again.

Evan walked out of Juliet's now empty office and down the hall to his own desk. There was no point going after her to convince her of his opinion, even if he knew he was right. Juliet still wasn't ready to hear or accept the truth—that she could still do this job if she'd just give herself a chance.

Not that Evan expected her to do it immediately. She wasn't ready to take those first steps back into active field-work, and that was fine. She should take all the time she needed to recover from what had happened to her.

He sat at his desk, pushing away the thoughts attempting to crowd into his mind. Images of Juliet lying bleeding on a warehouse floor, feebly trying to fend Evan off before she realized it was him and not the man who had attacked her.

In the middle of an undercover buy, the leader of a rival group, who didn't like that Bob and Lisa Sinclair were cutting in on his share of black-market profits, had forcefully taken Juliet in the middle of the night. Before Evan even knew what had happened, and could get to her, she had been horribly beaten and raped.

Every muscle in his body tensed. Even now, eighteen months later, Evan had a hard time just forming the words in his mind.

And that was part of the problem, wasn't it? They all—Evan, the Branson brothers, even Juliet herself—just tiptoed around it. Nobody ever really talked about it. He knew Juliet saw a shrink every once in a while, and was glad she did, but she never talked to anyone else about what had happened. Even though things didn't seem to be getting better for her, and maybe getting worse.

Evan sighed and leaned back in his chair. In order to make things easier for Juliet, they'd all agreed to her unspoken request not to talk about the attack. To give her time. But now, a year and a half later, they were doing the same thing: just agreeing and protecting and sheltering her. For example, supporting her in the choice to leave active field duty and embrace a desk job.

Honestly, that just made Evan mad, because he'd never known people less suited for a desk job than any member of the Branson family, Juliet included.

Juliet especially.

Evan had worked with her for years in the field and knew her instincts were unparalleled. She could read an undercover situation and formulate a plan—sometimes multiple plans—almost instantaneously. She could pinpoint the weakness of an organization or a person's individual psyche with frightening speed and accuracy.

More than once while undercover with her, Evan had been thankful she was a good guy, on his team, rather than vice versa. To say she was wasted as an analyst/handler wasn't exactly true; she was good at that, too. But she could be so much more.

Evan had no problem with Juliet taking the time she needed to heal from the physical and psychological wounds she had suffered last time she'd been undercover. As far as he was concerned she could take the rest of her life, if that's what she needed, and never set foot in the field again. He would be the first one to back her up in that decision. To hold her hand. To do more if she'd let him.

But what Evan couldn't stomach was that Juliet thought of herself as a *failure* as an undercover operative because of what had happened to her. That because she hadn't been able to escape her attacker, she'd failed.

Evan had tried multiple times to tell her what he had written in his official report of the incident. Even under the worst of possible circumstances, Juliet hadn't broken cover.

She'd saved multiple lives, his included, because of that. No one could've asked for more from her. Seasoned agents had broken under much less duress than Juliet had endured. But despite everything that happened to her even through the rape, Juliet hadn't told anyone she was law enforcement.

She was the furthest thing from a failure as an agent as possible. Evan wished he could make her understand that.

But Juliet no longer trusted herself. No longer considered becoming reinstated even a possibility. Because she believed she was—and always would be—a failure as an agent.

Evan knew he walked a fine line. He didn't want to push her for more than she was ready to take on, but knew that without some sort of push she might never move forward at all. Either way, it didn't matter. She wasn't ready right now, despite what he or anybody else said. Evan would just keep encouraging her, and hopefully, they'd find some way to ease her back in a few months from now.

Baby steps.

He needed to try to get Juliet to open up and talk about what was going on in her head, see if he could figure out a way to help her make some progress.

Of course, Evan couldn't throw stones too far while sitting in his glass house. He hadn't told anybody about the dreams that had been plaguing him for the past year and a half. Hadn't told anyone about how he sometimes sat in his car in front of Juliet's house at night, just to make sure she was safe.

In case she needed him to protect her. The way he hadn't been able to do on that last mission. The way that had haunted him ever since.

So maybe Juliet wasn't the only one who needed to make forward progress. Baby steps for him, too.

But right now he needed to get ready for his meeting with Vince Cady. He flipped through the files on his desk one more time.

Cady was a vicious bastard. Evan was delighted at the opportunity to slip inside his organization and wreak as much havoc as possible. He was a little mad that arresting Cady wasn't a priority for this operation, but understood why it wasn't. Omega always kept the big picture in mind.

A chair creaking at the desk across from his drew Evan's focus. Sawyer Branson winced a little as he took his arm out of the sling it had resided in for the past few weeks, and stretched it gently. "Ready for everything with Cady tomorrow?" he asked, rotating his shoulder.

Evan closed the files. "Yep. As much as I can be with this sort of thing. How's the arm?"

His friend grimaced. "Let's just say I don't recommend

getting shot. Even a flesh wound hurts like hell and takes a long time to heal. But it could've been much worse."

"And with pretty Dr. Megan now working right upstairs, I'll bet you're not even itching to get back out in the field." Evan tried not to snicker as he said it, but wasn't entirely successful.

Sawyer got that goofy smile at the mention of Megan Fuller, the same smile his brother Cameron got at the mention of his fiancée, Sophia Reardon.

Branson men were falling like flies around here. Evan couldn't help but grin.

"I'm not rushing the healing process, let's just say that," Sawyer said, stretching his arm out again. "Wouldn't want to have any permanent damage."

"Well, don't worry. I'll handle all the heavy lifting out in the field while you and Cameron play lover boys to your respective ladies."

Sawyer got serious. "You sure you feel all right about going in with Cady? Cam and I both feel we've left you on your own. Especially without Juliet available in this situation."

"I'll be fine. I've been doing most ops on my own for the past year now."

Neither of them mentioned why. Neither had to.

"Where are you meeting Cady tomorrow?" Sawyer asked after a moment's pause that held a novel's worth of unsaid words.

"Undetermined as of yet. I'm going to try to get him somewhere neutral. We'll see how it plays out."

"All right." Sawyer got up and put his arm back into the sling. "Keep us all posted."

"Yeah, it will be good to have Juliet as team leader on this one. She sees things nobody else does, sometimes."

Her brother nodded hesitantly. "Yeah, maybe. I hope so."

"She'll be fine, Sawyer. Safe here at Omega, as always."

Sawyer looked as if he might say something else, but didn't. He just nodded again, then began walking down the hall. "Hey, family barbecue next weekend. My mom says you better be there for this one or she's coming after you personally," he called over his shoulder.

"Yeah, okay, tell her I'll be there unless this case dictates otherwise." And the case would dictate otherwise; Evan would make sure of that. He loved the Branson family and their get-togethers. But until things were more comfortable between him and Juliet, he wouldn't be going. Juliet needed to know that her family was hers. Evan would never want to take that from her.

Evan read through the files one more time, familiarizing himself with every part of Vince Cady's operation. He would never let the drug lord know he had this sort of knowledge, of course. To Cady, Bob Sinclair would be a midlevel criminal: smart, but not too clever; industrious, but still a little lazy. Someone useful and nonthreatening.

Evan could admit it was easier when he'd had Juliet playing his wife. He'd just pretended to be in awe of her and head over heels in love. Nobody had ever had any difficulty buying that cover. Bob and Lisa Sinclair had made a good team. Everybody had accepted that Lisa was the brains of the couple and Bob was willing to do anything she asked. It made them seem appealing and adept, but not threatening.

Not threatening except to Robert Avilo, another midlevel criminal who didn't like how successful the Sinclairs had become in black-market buying and selling on what he considered to be his turf. In an attempt to get rid of the competition, to scare off the Sinclairs, Avilo had attacked Juliet.

Such a pity Avilo had died a few days after the attack

while resisting arrest. An arrest made based on an "anonymous" tip. Evan wished he could've killed the bastard himself. But he still took a little comfort knowing the man was dead and that Juliet would never have to see his face again.

And though she never broke cover even when raped by Avilo, Evan and Juliet had completely pulled out of the case after the attack. Juliet had been in the hospital and Evan had refused to leave her side. He had no idea what the word was on the street about why the Sinclairs hadn't been around for the past year and a half. Their disappearance had been pretty abrupt. But Evan took comfort in knowing that rumors floating about the Sinclairs would not be whispers that they were law enforcement.

Juliet, in her bravery and her silence, had seen to that.

But DS-13, the crime syndicate group, hadn't had any problems with Bob Sinclair's sudden reappearance when they'd contacted him last month. Neither had Vince Cady. Evan just hoped it stayed that way tomorrow, but knew he'd have to be ready for some questions.

He dumped onto his desk the contents of a large envelope he'd gotten from his filing cabinet earlier today. It contained items that had belonged to Bob Sinclair, and would help reestablish Evan's cover. A driver's license, of course. It had to be a real one that linked back to Bob Sinclair. There were too many online sites that, for a reasonable fee, could let Cady know if an ID was fake. So Bob Sinclair's license was real, complete with links to several unpaid parking tickets, and even arrests, when Bob had been younger. If a local cop ran his license or social security number—and it wasn't unreasonable to think that someone of Vince Cady's criminal caliber would have at least one police officer on his payroll—it would look real.

So would the credit cards in Sinclair's name, another way a cover could be easily blown if an operative wasn't careful. In today's technologically savvy world, credit cards that had never been used, or a social security number that could be traced back only a couple of years, were easily found and red-flagged. Bob Sinclair's credit cards had purchases and statements dating back ten years. It was some analyst's job at Omega to make sure all these electronically trackable items looked as real as possible. Whoever that person was did a damn good job.

The other items from the envelope included business cards for exporting companies and banks around the Baltimore and DC area. Even Sinclair's library card, randomly placed in his wallet. Plus two photographs. The first was of Bob and Lisa's wedding day. Evan and Juliet had posed outside a church, in wedding garb, hand in hand and smiling. Rice showered them in the picture, the perfect way to make it look as if a large crowd of people surrounded them. In actuality it had just been a few other agents, who had enjoyed pelting them with rice from every angle.

Evan picked up the other picture and studied it longer. He remembered that day from two years ago with crystal clarity. The photo had been taken in front of the Cape Henry Lighthouse on Chesapeake Bay in Virginia, during the winter. He and Juliet had driven there for the express purpose of getting this memento from the Sinclairs' secluded "honeymoon" so they could both have a copy in their wallet. A couple who posed as being in love with each other as much as Bob and Lisa did would definitely have pictures of each other with them at all times. Plus, it gave them added history, a more firm timeline.

Details like that could be the difference between life and death in an undercover operation.

For the photo, Evan had scooped Juliet up and cradled her in his arms. They'd asked a stranger to take their picture with their little disposable camera, explaining they were on their honeymoon. The stranger had gladly obliged, but had insisted Evan and Juliet seal the moment with a kiss.

The kiss had started out brief, just a staged moment for a picture. But then Evan had found he hadn't wanted to stop kissing Juliet. And judging by the way she clung to him, she hadn't wanted to stop, either. Her soft lips and warm mouth had been so different from the cold air that had surrounded them.

They had both totally forgotten about the stranger taking their picture, who evidently at some point had just left the camera on a nearby step and walked away, giving the "newlyweds" their privacy. When Evan and Juliet had finally broken apart, they'd both been breathing heavily. And had been confused as hell about what had just happened between them—so unexpected, but so perfectly right at the same time.

They'd been about to go undercover on a critical operation, however, so both of them had pushed whatever had just happened between them aside. Something to deal with later.

Of course, if Evan had known what would happen later, he would've made very different choices that day. He would have driven to the nearest hotel and made love with Juliet until neither of them could walk.

Evan took the credit cards and pictures and put them back into the wallet. Maybe it would've changed everything, maybe it would've changed nothing. He'd never know.

He took Bob Sinclair's wedding ring and slipped it on his finger. He might as well start getting used to its weight. He picked up the Saint Christopher necklace—Bob and Lisa had matching ones—and placed the chain around his neck. He kissed the medallion as Bob Sinclair had always done.

Evan stood and began packing everything away, straightening up his desk a little. If everything went the way they hoped, he wouldn't be here in Omega HQ very often over the next few days, for it would be too dangerous. He had done all he could do here at the office. He grabbed the keys to the SUV he'd be driving until the case was over.

It was time to slip on the Bob Sinclair persona. To think like him, walk like him, become him.

Chapter Five

Juliet found herself back at Omega Headquarters the next morning, early again. But for once her early arrival wasn't due to unreasonable fears and memories driving her from her home. Today she was in because she wanted to be, in order to provide Evan with any support he would need while meeting with Vince Cady.

She didn't expect there would be a whole lot she could do. Evan wouldn't be wearing a wire or transmitting device. No agent would take something like that to a first meeting with a perpetrator when he or she was sure to be searched; it would be a quick way to get killed. But if Evan needed any info, or advice Juliet could provide, she wanted to be there for his call.

She felt guilty enough for sending him in alone, but determined not to rehash all that again today. She would just do what she could from this end.

She stopped at the coffee shop down the block from Omega, ordered a cup of her favorite brew and made her way to the nondescript front doors of Sector Headquarters. The lobby of Omega could be mistaken for any financial or business building on the outskirts of Washington, DC. A security desk sat in front of the elevators. Everyone had to show their badges to get by. Nothing unusual.

But it was inside the elevators where the true security

started. A retinal and fingerprint scan, as well as an individualized code, were required before a passenger was taken to any secure floor. Nobody just walked off the streets and got into Omega.

It was the reason Juliet felt safe here, when she didn't anywhere else.

The morning ended up being as uneventful as she had hoped. She sat at her desk, monitoring all calls and electronic submissions that might be coming from Evan. But except for a brief text stating the meeting was confirmed for 11:00 a.m. near the Baltimore Pier, they hadn't heard anything from him. No news wasn't necessarily good news in this business, but it wasn't necessarily bad news, either.

Juliet forced herself to relax. She'd feel better once Evan's initial meeting with Vince Cady was complete. So much rode on this one event.

Her brother Sawyer stuck his head in the door. "Heard from Karcz?"

"A couple of hours ago. Everything seemed good. Meeting scheduled for eleven." Juliet looked down at the clock on one of the computer screens she had open. Five minutes to eleven. Moment of truth.

"Cam and I are headed into DC proper. Bomb threat issue and the Bureau needs some extra hands. All available agents are headed in."

Juliet nodded. "Okay. Well, I've definitely got it covered here. Just waiting for Evan to check in after the meeting. Nothing I can really do except wait. But in case he needs any emergency info I want to be standing by."

"Okay, sis. We'll be on cell phone silence because of the bomb threat. FBI on the scene is concerned that the perps might be using a cell to detonate, so they're jamming all frequencies."

"I'll figure something out if I need you. I'm expecting a boring day."

Sawyer left and Juliet went back to her work. One computer actively monitored the Baltimore Police Department. They had no idea what was going on with this case, so could actually stumble in and do harm if she wasn't careful. She'd give them info on a need-to-know basis, if it looked as if they might interfere with the case somehow. She'd also been reading through the files of Vince Cady's known associates all morning. Nothing terribly interesting there, either, but Juliet wanted to make sure she was up to speed on all the names and faces.

She almost missed it. Amid the chaos of the monitors and files, hypervigilant in her effort to make sure she could provide any support Evan might need—overcompensating for guilt much?—Juliet almost missed the single communiqué that could bring the entire operation crashing down.

It was an automated email from the Omega system. It had filtered through the Virginia courts and correction system, and provided a list of three people who had been released from a Richmond jail on bond this morning at eight o'clock. Omega's system only red-flagged info concerning criminals or suspects in their database—people Omega had caught, were currently trying to catch, or planned to catch in the future.

The system listed one of the releases, a low-level hired thug named Mark Bolick, because of the agent who had apprehended the suspect: Evan Karcz. At first Juliet didn't pay the communiqué any attention. As an analyst, she had multiple lists like this come across her computer screen every day.

Mark Bolick had been arrested last month during an altercation between the crime group DS-13 and some Omega agents, a situation that had almost left her brother Sawyer dead. Most of the members of DS-13, including the dirty ex-FBI agent running the crime ring, had been killed. But some had been arrested, including Bolick. Evan had been undercover, not directly involved in the case. But because Sawyer, the agent in charge, had been in critical condition, Evan had arrested the remaining bad guys. Not common practice in undercover work.

Mark Bolick in and of himself wasn't much of a problem. Juliet didn't know why he was getting out on bail so early and didn't really care. The problem was Bolick had ties to Vince Cady, based on information she'd read in the files this morning. Although he didn't seem to be a big part of Cady's organization, he was dating Cady's niece.

It didn't take a genius to figure out that Bolick, after sitting in jail for over a month, would be heading up to Baltimore as soon as possible, probably to see his girlfriend. But it wasn't a stretch to think he might check in with Cady immediately.

And he'd be sure to remember the man posing as Bob Sinclair as the one who had arrested him just a few weeks before. That would mean the end of the case for Evan.

And probably his life, especially if they'd already discussed any details about anything. Or maybe just because Cady or one of his men would see it as an opportunity to get rid of an undercover cop.

Juliet immediately speed dialed Evan's phone. A call was risky, but at least produced immediate communication. Evan would be able to talk his way out of it, make up some excuse to Cady about why he was taking the call.

But he didn't answer.

Juliet immediately sent a text from her computer to the

same number. Aunt Suzie had a heart attack. Mom needs you to come home right away.

Aunt Suzie was the signal for general emergency. Come home right away meant to get out of there now. Evan wouldn't have any details, but he would know what the message meant.

Juliet sat staring at her computer, waiting for the screen to give a received message. All Omega-issued phones had the capacity to show if a message had been received. Helpful, but not foolproof, since it couldn't notify the handler if the *agent* was the one who had actually read the text. Just that it had been accessed.

Juliet didn't necessarily expect Evan to respond, depending on what was going on in the meeting with Cady, but she did want to know the warning had been received.

But nothing. She sent the text again, just to be sure. Still nothing.

Multiple scenarios ran through her head ranging from the benign—Evan was in a momentary situation where he couldn't access his phone or didn't have a signal—to the catastrophic—he had already been exposed as an undercover agent and executed by Vince Cady.

Juliet gave it five more minutes, sending the message three more times.

Nothing.

She looked at her watch and did some quick calculations. Eleven-fifteen. Evan should definitely already be meeting with Cady by now. And it was a hundred fifty miles from Richmond to Baltimore, so it was conceivable that Mark Bolick could've already made it there, too. She needed to find out where Evan was and get in touch with him.

Juliet opened the program that allowed her to use

Evan's phone as a tracker. She entered in the code for it and waited.

Device not found.

Juliet entered in the code one more time to be sure. Nothing again. Now she really began to worry. There were too many unknowns in this situation. She had to make a decision. She didn't want to blow the operation for nothing, but neither was she willing to risk Evan's life.

She called the contact number she had for the Baltimore PD. Quickly she explained the situation to a ranking officer there, asking him to send out a unit to check the location of Evan's meeting with Cady near the Baltimore Pier, explaining the need for speed but also stealth, if possible. The officer assured her of their cooperation and that he would call back shortly.

It didn't take long, about fifteen minutes—although it felt much longer—for the officer to call her back. His response had Juliet immediately running down the hall to Burgamy's office.

"Dennis, we have a problem with Evan in the undercover op," she told her supervisor, without any preamble. She explained about Mark Bolick.

"Have you contacted Baltimore PD and GPS for his phone?"

"Yes, for both. I'm not getting any GPS location reading for his phone at all. BPD sent a unit to the location I provided, where Evan reported the meeting with Vince Cady would be held, but no one was there. They said it was completely empty, with no sign of any sort of struggle or foul play."

Burgamy stood. "Okay, that's both good and bad."

Juliet knew what he meant. Evan wasn't lying in a pool

of blood somewhere, so that was good. But they had no idea where he was, and no way of contacting him. That was bad.

Very bad.

"It's just a matter of time before Mark Bolick shows up while Evan is there." Juliet tried not to pace around Burgamy's office, but it was difficult.

"Have Baltimore put out an APB on Bolick. Maybe we can catch him before he meets up with Cady and Evan. If he's in Baltimore, he's breaking his bond agreement, anyway, by being out of state."

Juliet had her phone out to make the call.

Burgamy stopped her. "Juliet, you worked with Evan as this persona before. Do you know of any places he might have suggested to Cady? Neutral places that would make the guy more comfortable? Obviously, the meeting wasn't going as well as Evan hoped if they aren't at the location they agreed to, and his phone is completely offline."

This probably wouldn't have happened if you'd gone undercover with him.

Burgamy didn't say the words out loud, and may not have even been thinking them. But Juliet could feel them floating in the air. Maybe it was just her own guilt talking.

"I don't know. Yeah. Maybe a couple of places." Juliet could picture a few.

"I don't have any agents to send out. Everybody has gone into DC to help with this bomb issue. Until we know for sure Evan is in trouble, the bomb has to be my priority."

Juliet nodded. Burgamy was right; he couldn't pull men off a known crisis for something that was only a possible one. "Okay, I'll work with Baltimore PD. Hopefully this is just some sort of fluke thing and Evan will be in touch soon."

But her gut told her the opposite.

Chapter Six

From the very beginning this meeting with Vince Cady hadn't gone the way Evan had hoped. It had started okay, a call with an agreed meeting time and place at an empty office building near the Baltimore Pier. The location allowed for privacy, but also a measure of safety for Cady. It would be easy to disappear into the nearby crowds if a quick getaway was needed.

Evan had reported the meeting location to Omega, then had shown up, ready for Bob Sinclair to be anything and everything the drug lord needed him to be. But Cady wasn't there. Evan had waited fifteen minutes, wondering with each minute that passed if the entire operation was a failure before it even began, before two thugs had shown up.

"Where's Cady?" he had asked.

Neither had answered, just walked up to him and began frisking him. Thank God he wasn't wearing a wire.

"I don't have a weapon," Evan had told them during the pat-down. That had been a conscious decision. In some undercover ops he did carry a weapon, because that's what the persona would do. But Bob Sinclair was a buyer and seller, not muscle for hire. In most situations, he wouldn't have a weapon.

Although Evan sort of wished Bob had one now.

The thugs took his cell phone from his pocket and one walked outside with it. Then the other guy, still not saying a word, pulled out his own phone and dialed a number.

He handed the device to Evan.

"Um, hello?"

"Mr. Sinclair, this is Vince Cady."

"I thought we were meeting here at the pier, Mr. Cady." Evan tried to put just the right amount of annoyance into his tone. Bob Sinclair would want Vince Cady's business, but would not be desperate for it.

"Yes, well, we've had a slight change in plans for security purposes. I felt this was necessary, since we have never actually met."

"Okay, so what's the new plan?"

"Now that I know we are talking on a secure line and that no one else can hear us, I was hoping we could come up with a new meeting location."

This wasn't totally unreasonable. It seemed as if Cady was a suspicious bastard, but that was probably why he was still in business.

Evan thought fast. Juliet could still use his phone to track him, but if he could suggest somewhere he was familiar with, that would at least give Evan a slight advantage. Being outnumbered and unarmed was disadvantage enough.

"Fine. There's a group of warehouses near the Francis Scott Key Bridge." Evan gave Cady the address. "It's neutral and private. Let's meet there."

"Sounds fine, Mr. Sinclair. My associates will escort you. And I will gladly replace your phone. Sorry for the inconvenience."

Evan was about to ask what he meant, but Cady had already disconnected.

"I guess we're going to the Francis Scott Key Bridge," Evan told the man putting the phone away.

"Mr. Cady said there would be two of you."

Evan didn't blink an eye. "Not today. The wife couldn't make it."

The other thug walked in from outside. "Okay, it's done. Are we ready?"

"Can I get my phone back now?" Evan asked him.

"No. It's on its way to the bottom of the harbor. Sorry." The man didn't look a bit sorry.

Damn. This meant Evan was totally on his own. Unless Omega had developed some super tracking software in the past six hours, his only contact with them was now a plaything for fishes.

The ride to the warehouse near the Francis Scott Key Bridge was uneventful. Less than uneventful, almost completely silent.

"I left my Jeep in hourly parking. Between my cell phone in the harbor and our little field trip, this is turning into an expensive day."

Nothing. Evan gave up on trying to engage them.

The warehouses were what Evan remembered. A large area of identical buildings, almost all empty, surrounded by industrial structures. It would be easy to get lost, or end up in the wrong warehouse if you didn't know exactly where you were going. Multiple ways leading in and out. Helpful for people who didn't like being hemmed in. He and Juliet had done business at this very location as Bob and Lisa Sinclair.

A door to one of the empty warehouses stood open and they drove straight in. There stood Vince Cady, leaning casually against his SUV, surrounded by four of his closest buddies. Evan got out of the car as it stopped.

"Mr. Sinclair." Cady walked toward him and shook his

hand. The man was in his midfifties, with salt-and-pepper hair, short and trim. "It is good to finally meet you. I am sorry for all the subterfuge and drama of switching locations."

"You've got to have security measures. I understand."

"And where is the lovely Mrs. Sinclair I've heard so much about?"

Evan hadn't expected Cady to start asking about Juliet this early. "She's not here."

"I can see that. *Why* is she not here with you?"

"Lisa and I don't do business together anymore." Evan tried to keep it as broad and simple as possible.

Cady stared at him for a long moment, one eyebrow raised. "I don't like unexpected changes, Mr. Sinclair. I was told you and Mrs. Sinclair always worked together. That you were the brawn and she was the brains of your partnership, no offense intended."

Evan gave his most easygoing smile. "Well, now I'm both the brawn and the brains of the operation. Nothing has to go through a committee."

But Cady didn't seem interested in Evan's friendly demeanor. "From what I understand, Mrs. Sinclair has not been seen for quite a long time. Over a year in fact."

Evan shrugged. Cady knew more than Omega had thought. Evan didn't want to give away any info by blabbering. "We went our separate ways. So what?"

"I had heard such good things about you, Mr. Sinclair. About you and Mrs. Sinclair as a team." Cady turned and walked back toward his men, who were standing by the car a few feet away. Evan was very well aware that he was in the middle of a warehouse surrounded by Vince Cady's thugs. Highly armed ones.

And he had no weapon and no backup coming.

"But I'd also heard a few rumors, too. Rumors that

you might be law enforcement and that Mrs. Sinclair was no longer with you because she'd found out that fact and left." Now surrounded safely by his men, Cady turned back and faced Evan. "I so hoped she'd be with you today so that those rumors could be put to rest. But she isn't, and I have no choice but to believe that you aren't who you say you are."

So much for not worrying about any rumors surrounding the Sinclairs' absence. Suddenly Evan found six weapons pointed directly at him.

"That makes you a loose end. Unfortunately, I don't allow any loose ends."

JULIET HADN'T BEEN SURE exactly where she was going in Baltimore when she jumped into her car not long after talking with Burgamy; she just knew she couldn't stay in the office. The Baltimore PD was being less than helpful, although, in their defense, Juliet wasn't sure exactly what she was asking them to do.

Look for someone, somewhere in your city, who may be in danger, but may be perfectly fine.

Baltimore law enforcement had their own problems, and right now Evan Karcz wasn't one of them.

They had put out the APB on Mark Bolick. And thanks to some cameras she'd accessed showing Bolick leaving the courthouse that morning, she knew what he was driving and his license plate.

Given all that information, the chances of Bolick getting picked up by the police were pretty good. But the chances of that happening before he blew Evan's cover were much slimmer.

She would start at the pier. Maybe there was something the officers had missed. Northern DC to Baltimore was only forty-five minutes. Juliet was already halfway there.

But the call came in before she ever reached the pier. Juliet's heart stopped just for a moment when she saw it was her contact at the Baltimore PD. She put the phone on speaker and answered it, still driving.

"Agent Branson—"

Juliet didn't bother to correct him about the incorrect agent title.

"—the vehicle from the APB you had us put out has been spotted. A uniform radioed it in, but then was called to a nearby emergency and so wasn't able to pursue."

Damn it. "Okay. Was the vehicle seen near the pier?"

"No, near the Francis Scott Key Bridge."

As soon as Juliet heard the words she swerved across two lanes to reach the exit from the highway, ignoring the angry honks from other drivers.

She was just a few minutes from the FSK Bridge, southeast of Baltimore. The officer gave her the last known whereabouts of Bolick's car. Not far from the warehouses she and Evan had used for some buys when they'd worked together.

Had he moved the meeting out here? If so, why hadn't he let them know? Of course, it was possible that Mark Bolick was in this area for an entirely different reason that had nothing to do with Vince Cady or Evan. Or that the car the officer saw was the wrong one or no longer held Bolick.

Juliet's familiarity with the roads near the warehouses helped her as she navigated. But the area was large and there were lots of places to stay hidden if someone was trying to. That was one of the reasons she and Evan had chosen it for use in their undercover work.

She spotted Bolick's car, with him still driving it, thank goodness, as it pulled up in front of one of the warehouses. Juliet cursed under her breath. Vince Cady must be around here somewhere and Bolick was about to walk in on his meeting with Evan. It was too late to call for any sort of backup, and if she tried to arrest Bolick right here, he might yell and tip Cady off. She needed to do something more drastic.

Juliet pulled in behind Bolick as he was getting out of his vehicle, glad that the relaxed dress code at Omega made her look less like law enforcement. She didn't let herself think about what she was doing, just threw her car keys under the floor mat, grabbed her Glock 9 mm out of the glove compartment and slid it into the back waistband of her jeans as she quickly opened her own door. She grabbed some papers resting on the passenger seat.

Bolick wasn't a big guy, thank goodness.

"Hi. Excuse me? Sir?" Juliet ruffled through the papers as she got out of her car. "I'm so sorry. I'm completely lost."

"I can't help you, lady." Bolick made no move toward her, didn't even look at her, but Juliet didn't let that deter her. She kept walking.

"I just need to figure out where I am, based on this address. My phone died—"

"Sorry. I don't know anything about this area." Bolick turned away and began heading for the warehouse door. Juliet rushed to catch up with him.

"Can you just look at this?" She touched him on the arm and he turned, scowling. Juliet didn't wait to see what he would do next. She hit him in the chin with a brisk uppercut, putting her weight behind the punch, before he could get a good look at her.

She caught Bolick as he crumpled to the ground, just as she had expected.

Juliet could feel her entire body shaking as she dragged him the few feet to the trunk of his car. She got the keys out of his pocket and unlocked it, using all her strength to heft his unconscious form and roll him in. She knew he wouldn't be out forever, so grabbed some duct tape from her own car and tied his hands and covered his mouth. Then she got into his car and drove it a couple blocks away, where it couldn't be seen.

Juliet walked back to the warehouse, adrenaline still pooling through her entire body. Hopefully, the threat to Evan had passed, because she didn't think she could possibly be any help to him at this moment even if he needed it. She clenched her jaw in an attempt to stop her teeth from chattering. Mark Bolick was the closest she'd come to any sort of physical altercation—hell, almost any physical contact—with a stranger since her attack.

Juliet crouched down, focusing on her breathing and getting in as much oxygen as possible. Eventually, her hands stopped shaking and her heart rate settled into a less frantic pace. She made a call to Omega, reporting the location of Bolick's car and that he could be found in the trunk. Someone from headquarters would handle it and make sure Bolick was kept out of the picture while Evan was undercover with Cady.

Feeling a little better, she stood up. Her job here was finished, right? Mark Bolick no longer posed a threat to Evan's mission, so she was free to return to the safety of the Omega offices. Juliet began walking toward her car, but then stopped abruptly.

She couldn't just leave. Yes, Bolick was out of the picture, but she couldn't just go, not knowing if Evan was okay. Why couldn't he be reached? Why couldn't they track his phone? Juliet knew she would never be able to forgive herself if he was in trouble and she had left him to run back to safety.

Observe. That's all she had to do. She wouldn't need to make her presence known. She wouldn't interfere. She'd just make sure nobody was about to kill Evan or anything like that.

And if he *was* in trouble? Then she'd call for backup. Juliet took out her phone. As a matter of fact, she'd call Omega right now, let them know her status and get Baltimore PD on standby if necessary. Done. She could do this.

Keeping her breath slow and even, Juliet turned and began walking back toward the warehouse, deciding to go to a rear door she knew each of these buildings contained. She rubbed her damp palms on the thighs of her jeans as she silently made her way along the wall, her weapon still tucked in the waistband under her lightweight sweater.

She just prayed she wouldn't have to use it. And if she did, that she wouldn't freeze up. Sweat broke out on her forehead just thinking about it.

Juliet opened the door to the warehouse as silently as possible. She could hear some people talking, but couldn't make out the words. She eased inside.

She wasn't prepared for the hand that grabbed her shoulder from behind. She stopped. Everything stopped.

Her movements, her thoughts, her breathing, even her heartbeat—it all stopped. Neither fight nor flight was an option. She had forgotten how to do both.

She felt the cold muzzle of a weapon against the back of her neck and realized it didn't matter, she couldn't do either, anyway. So much for just observing.

"What are you doing here?" the man said from behind her.

Juliet fought to get a grip on her terror. "N-nothing," she stammered. "I got lost."

He used his free hand to push her, face forward, against the door she'd just closed. She sucked in a breath, gasping for air, her skin clammy. Squeezed her eyes shut and struggled to withhold a whimper as the man began running his hand down her back.

Juliet felt bile rise in her throat at his touch. She might vomit right here. Her shudders returned full force.

Blessedly, the hand stopped when it reached the Glock tucked in her jeans.

"What's this?" he barked close to her ear. She cringed, unable to answer even if she had a good plan for what to say. Which she very definitely didn't.

"Thomas, what's going on back there?" a voice from the center of the warehouse called out.

"I found an intruder, Mr. Cady. A woman coming in through the back door."

Juliet tried to calm her breathing enough to listen for Evan's voice, but couldn't manage it. She was spending all her energy attempting to control her panic.

Her captor grabbed her arm and began dragging her toward the middle of the warehouse. Juliet didn't resist much, especially when they rounded a stack of boxes and she could see what was going on with Cady and his men.

She expected to find weapons trained at her, but found them pointed in the opposite direction.

At Evan.

Juliet had to give him credit; he kept his wits about him even with her showing up so unexpectedly. She couldn't figure out what to say, just stared at Evan as the man holding her arm steered her closer to the group.

Evan sighed dramatically and rolled his eyes.

"Damn it, Lisa, I thought we agreed you were going to stay out of sight at the pier. What the hell are you doing here?"

Chapter Seven

Evan knew he was taking a huge risk engaging Juliet as Lisa Sinclair, but didn't see any other choice. Cady didn't trust Bob Sinclair, thinking it suspicious that he was here without his "wife." Well, she was here now.

Why Juliet was, Evan had no idea. She should be behind a desk at Omega, where she felt safe. What the hell was going on?

Juliet seemed only a moment away from complete panic, if her expression was anything to go by. She pulled as far as she could from the man holding her arm. Evan knew she didn't like anyone touching her, and was sure that went double for some thug she didn't know.

"Cady, have your guy let her go. My wife doesn't like to be manhandled."

Cady nodded at the man and he released her. She floundered for just a second, not seeming to know what to do, but then rushed over to Evan. He put his arm around her—loosely, so she wouldn't feel trapped—and slid her behind him. Keeping himself between her and the guns still pointed his way.

Vince Cady chuckled. "Looks like you haven't quite been honest with me, Bob. You made me think your lovely wife had left you for good. Yet here she is."

"Yeah, well, she wasn't supposed to be."

"And why is that?"

Juliet still didn't seem to be capable of any sort of speech, so Evan just kept talking, well aware of all the weapons trained on them. "She was supposed to stay at the car, back at the pier. Away from all this, and people throwing her around." Evan gestured toward the guy who had brought her into the warehouse.

"She was armed, Mr. Cady. I didn't know why she was here," the guy chirped, holding Juliet's Glock out as proof.

"Lisa is always armed," Evan interjected quickly. He didn't want to take a chance on Cady linking the words *armed* and *law enforcement* together. "She had an…accident a while ago and feels better carrying a gun with her." Evan could feel Juliet stiffen behind him, but couldn't do anything to make her more comfortable. He shrugged and smiled at Cady. "I personally find an armed woman very sexy."

Cady looked at Evan and Juliet for a long moment, then gave the motion—finally—for his men to lower their weapons. Evan felt a little better, but knew they were still far from safe.

"Yes, that was another rumor I heard about your wife. That someone had tried to kill her," Cady declared.

Evan gave a curt nod. "We don't like to talk about it. But Lisa and I decided she would stay out of the business side of things after that incident."

"And yet here she is at our meeting." Cady's eyebrow was raised.

"Not by my choice." Now that the guns were no longer pointed at them, Evan drew Juliet from behind him and wrapped his arm around her. He could feel fine trembles racking her body. "She must have gotten a little scared and followed us when you decided to switch the location. Is that right, honey?"

Evan looked down at Juliet and squeezed her closer, trying to get a reaction from her. She nodded blankly. Not great, but enough.

He pulled her even nearer to his side. "Look, Mr. Cady, ever since Lisa got attacked she's been a little skittish. She doesn't like being touched by people she doesn't know, and she doesn't like being surrounded by a roomful of men with weapons. That's why we've been keeping a low profile for the past few months."

Evan hated using Juliet's attack as a tactic to get ahead in this situation, but didn't see any way around it.

Cady broke into a smile. "Trying to keep your woman safe. No wonder you were acting so suspiciously! I can totally respect that. I am a family man myself. I have a wife who means a great deal to me, as yours obviously does to you."

For the first time, Cady's men seemed to relax, as if they finally believed their boss was okay with the situation. Evan smiled also. "Exactly."

"Thomas, give Mrs. Sinclair back her gun. She obviously doesn't feel safe without it."

"But, Mr. Cady, are you sure you want her to have a weapon?"

"These people aren't our enemy, Thomas." Cady gestured to Juliet. "Would you feel better about this situation if you had your gun back?"

Juliet nodded.

"But please don't shoot poor Thomas. He was just doing his job."

She nodded again. When her captor walked over and handed Juliet the Glock, she kept it in her hand, down at her side. Evan could tell she felt much better having it in her possession, although the lack of color in her face still worried him.

It was a nice gesture on Cady's part to give Juliet the security blanket she so obviously needed, although Evan was sure the man's motives were not altruistic. He was trying to form some sort of bond between them. But Evan was also aware that there were at least four men in the room who could kill both him and Juliet immediately if she began to raise her weapon in a threatening manner. Having the gun in her hand provided a slim facade of control at best.

"I'm sorry for what happened to you, Mrs. Sinclair." Cady bowed his head slightly. "I would never condone that sort of behavior from any employees of mine."

"All right, Cady, let's cut the chitchat. You have some surface-to-air missiles to sell. I have a buyer, possibly multiple buyers, who are interested."

"Good, good. I also have other items, much more important items, to be auctioned off. Including something acquired only recently."

"More important than SAMs?" Evan raised an eyebrow. "I find that hard to believe."

"How about access to override codes that would allow someone to turn US military drones onto any target they so desire. Attacks untraceable back to them."

Evan swallowed the expletive he so desperately wanted to let loose. Instead he gave an impressed whistle through his teeth. "You have drone override codes available for sale?"

Cady had the gall to casually flick a piece of lint off his shirt. "I do, in fact."

"Wow!" Evan feigned excitement. "That's some next level stuff. Where did you get them?"

"I'm sure your buyers would not actually care, correct? They would only want to be sure that the codes work."

Evan could feel Juliet stiffen beside him. How the hell

did Cady have drone override codes in his possession? Things had just gone from bad to critical.

Evan sure as hell cared where and how Cady had gotten the codes, but Bob Sinclair wouldn't press. Evan had to let it go. "That's true, and it's also pretty impressive, Mr. Cady. I was worried that since DS-13 seemed to be out of business, there would be a gap in merchandise available for sale. But it seems that's not the case at all. As long as everything works, I'm sure my buyers will be interested, no matter where the codes came from."

"I'm glad to hear that. I plan to have an auction on Monday. A few choice buyers, you included. I will be in touch with more details."

Monday. That was only three days away.

Cady walked over and held out his hand. Evan reluctantly unwrapped his arm from around Juliet to shake it. She still didn't seem too steady on her feet and he knew he needed to get her out of here as soon as possible. He willed her to stay strong.

"Like I said, I am a family man," Cady told Evan. "One of the reasons I contacted you in the first place is because the two of you work together as a couple. Call me a romantic, but I find that love makes people more trustworthy."

Cady turned to Juliet. "I know you don't enjoy the business any longer, but I hope that you will see coming to my home as more than business. I can promise your safety."

Evan didn't like where this was heading. "Mr. Cady—"

The man stepped back from them. "In any case, my invitation to the auction at my house is for you as a pair. If your lovely wife decides she cannot make it, there is no reason for you to come, either, Mr. Sinclair. My wife will be expecting a couple, not a single man. I am not interested in letting her down on this matter."

"I just think it would be better—"

"Both or neither, Mr. Sinclair." Cady seemed uninterested in any argument, so Evan just shut his mouth.

The drug lord turned and began walking toward his men. "I assume, since your wife had to arrive in some sort of vehicle, you won't need my men to escort you back to the pier."

Evan looked down at Juliet, who nodded again. "Yes, we've got our own ride, thanks."

"Then I'll be in touch and look forward to seeing you both again soon." Cady and his men walked out the door.

EVAN WATCHED THEM LEAVE, then tucked Juliet more firmly to his side. "Hang in there, baby," he whispered.

"Evan, I can't..." Her voice was barely more than a whisper.

"Don't think about anything right now. Let's just get out to your car. Where is it?"

"In the back alley, on the northeast side of the building." Her words had an uneven cadence.

Evan led her out through the door she'd come in. They made it to her car.

If possible Juliet looked even more pale out in the sunlight. Evan leaned her up against the vehicle "Where are the keys, Jules? Under the mat?"

She nodded.

"Okay. Let's get you in the car and back home. All right?"

"Evan, I'm going to be s—" Juliet didn't even get all the words out before she bent over and was violently ill all over the pavement.

Evan offered his support by touching her back, but she waved him away. Even after she lost the contents of her stomach she continued to dry heave.

Evan knew there was nothing he could do. Her system

was in shock and just needed to run its course. He winced as she once again heaved. It was painful to watch, and he was just glad she had been able to keep herself under control for so long.

Eventually Juliet pulled herself to an upright position, although she kept her arms wrapped tightly around her stomach. "I think I'm okay now." Her voice was cracked and hoarse.

Evan helped her into the car, thankful that her face had some color in it now and the shaking seemed to have stopped.

"Juliet, what the hell are you doing here?" he finally asked, as they pulled away from the warehouse area and headed back toward DC.

She sat with her eyes closed, leaning back against the headrest. "Mark Bolick, one of the guys you arrested from DS-13 last month with Sawyer, has ties to Cady and was about to blow your cover."

Evan cursed under his breath. Things had already been going pretty poorly before Juliet arrived. If Bolick had stumbled in and accused him of being a cop, that would've been it for Evan.

"You saved my life," he told Juliet.

She gave a bark of mirthless laughter. "Not on purpose. If there had been anyone else around I could've called, I would have, believe me."

"Well, you did it and that's what counts. Plus, Cady was pretty antsy about why Lisa Sinclair wasn't with me. You showing up when you did probably saved my life again, or at the very least the whole case."

Juliet still had her eyes closed. "Like I said, I didn't do that on purpose, either. Then I almost blew the whole thing."

"But you didn't."

She shrugged and Evan knew better than to argue with her. She refused to acknowledge her own success because of her physical reaction afterward.

"You did good, Jules. It was a dicey situation. Cady was ready to call the whole thing off, or maybe even get rid of me completely, because you weren't there."

"I thought you had a plan for what you were going to say."

Evan took the exit for the interstate leading to Washington. "I had a bunch of possibilities, based on how the situation was going. But Cady started up about you almost right away. I was still reeling from the change of locations and my phone sinking to the bottom of the harbor."

"No wonder we couldn't contact you. I tried to let you know about Bolick, then sent Baltimore PD to the pier."

"Evidently, Cady's even more security-conscious than we thought. And definitely pro-family. He was not interested in talking to me at all if you weren't in the picture. Every excuse I had—that we had broken up, that you just weren't interested in the business anymore—wasn't going to fly, I could tell."

Out of the corner of his eye, Evan could see tension fill Juliet's body and her breathing become more rapid, although she was still leaning against the headrest.

"What? Are you okay? Are you going to be sick again?"

"Evan, Cady's not going to deal with you if I'm not involved."

He reached over and took her hand, shocked when she didn't jerk away instantly. He had touched Juliet more in the past hour than he had in the whole past year.

"It'll be all right, Jules. I can make it work without you."

Now Juliet opened her pretty green eyes to look at him, her breathing becoming even more pronounced. "How, Evan? You heard Cady. He was *adamant* about the two of us being together or you not bothering to come to the auction at all. And he has drone override codes."

Juliet was right. Despite his assurances, Evan couldn't see how he was going to make it into the auction without her. If he had known what a hangup Cady would have for Juliet's attendance with him, Evan would've gotten another agent—someone who could pass for Juliet—and gone in with her. Sure, that plan had its own problems, but it was better than where they were now: having an open invitation to infiltrate a huge crime lord's organization, but not being able to move on it.

Evan cursed silently. He couldn't force Juliet to go back undercover; after what he'd seen today, he knew the price would be too high.

And honestly, despite the confidence he had in her overall, and the firm belief she could again become the great agent she had once been, he wasn't sure she could do it right now. Not that she was willing, anyway.

Evan glanced over at Juliet, watching her trying to get herself under control. She didn't look like a law enforcement agent right now. She looked like a woman who was frightened. She still had her Glock clutched in her small fist.

He would just have to find another way to get into the auction with Vince Cady. But hell if he had a single damned idea of how he would do so.

He felt Juliet slip her hand out of his as she turned her head to the window. Silence permeated the car. Evan didn't know what he could possibly say to make this better, so he didn't even try.

They drove all the way back to DC—Evan would have to send someone else to get his car at the pier—and pulled into the Omega parking garage without Juliet saying another word. At one point Evan had wondered if she'd fallen asleep. But at least her breathing was even and she had color in her face. All signs of her earlier panic attack seemed to be gone.

Maybe that was why he was so shocked when she turned to him as he parked her car.

"I'll go back under, Evan. It's our only hope."

Chapter Eight

"We sat in this very room yesterday and had this exact conversation. You weren't ready then. You can't possibly be ready now."

Sawyer spoke to Juliet, but wasn't looking at her; he was glaring at Evan. The conversation had been going on for the past twenty minutes. It was the first time in memory that Juliet could recall wishing that a bomber still threatened Washington, DC.

At least then her brothers wouldn't be here trying to convince her of something she already knew: this was a bad idea.

"Sawyer, it's the only option." Juliet didn't raise her voice.

"Hell no, it's not the only option. And even if it was, we'd figure out something else."

Silence flooded the room. That was the problem—there really weren't any other options. Not ones that could solve the problem in the amount of time they had. None of the four people in the room, Juliet, Evan, Sawyer or Cameron, had much that could be offered by way of an alternate plan.

Juliet spoke calmly. "It was bad enough when Cady had the surface-to-air missiles. But now he has the drone override codes. If anyone has an alternate plan I'm willing to listen to it. If not..."

More silence. Which was broken by the phone ringing on the conference room table.

"Why did a call get routed in here?" Evan asked.

"Because it's Dylan. I gave him a heads-up and told him to call." Sawyer looked at Juliet, eyebrow raised.

She could feel her nostrils flare; she couldn't believe they had brought their oldest brother into this. This was her decision, not theirs. She slammed her palm over the handset before Cameron could pick it up. "You know what you two are? Tattletales."

Cameron brushed her hand away and pressed the button for the speakerphone. "Hey, Dylan."

Dylan had been an Omega agent for a long time before getting out a few years ago to start his own charter airplane business in the western part of Virginia. He wasn't one to beat around the bush. "What's going on, Jules?"

There were few people in the world Juliet had more respect for than her oldest brother. He, more than anyone else knew the price of undercover work. "It looks like I need to go back under, Dylan. As Lisa Sinclair."

Dylan knew what had happened eighteen months before. Juliet didn't need to explain it to him. "Do you want to do it?" he asked.

"I think saying I *want* to do it would be a gross overstatement. But I don't think there's any way around it. Vince Cady has somehow acquired drone override codes, Dyl."

Juliet could hear him whistle through his teeth. He knew the ramifications of having these codes in the wrong hands.

"Evan, are you there?" Dylan finally asked.

"Yeah, man, I'm here."

"What happened today? How did Juliet even get drawn into this?"

Evan explained about Bolick, playing up the part about

Juliet knocking him unconscious and locking him in his own trunk. Then he told about Cady's proclivity for hiring people who had family, or at least loved ones, and how the criminal wasn't interested in Evan coming in as a single man working alone.

"Sounds like Juliet was caught unawares in this situation," Dylan stated plainly. "You felt like she handled everything all right?"

Juliet wasn't offended by her brother's question to Evan. He could give a much more accurate description of what happened.

Evan looked at her. "She held it together. Everything was dicey for a while, but she didn't blow our cover. Although I can definitely attest she wasn't having a good time."

He conveniently left out the part about her throwing up all over the place as soon as they got out of the warehouse. That wouldn't reassure anyone.

"Evan, it's your life on the line, too, if you go under together. Are you sure this is what you want?" Dylan asked.

"Look, Dylan, I'll be honest. If we had a bunch of other choices, I would weigh them all before throwing Juliet back into this. But we don't, so there's not much point in talking hypotheticals."

Dylan's days as an Omega team leader were clearly evident in his voice as he said, "But do you believe the objective is obtainable if you and Juliet resume cover?"

"Honestly, I don't know." Evan shook his head. "But without her, at this point, we have a zero percent chance for success."

Dylan's sigh was tired.

Juliet had been glaring at her brothers as the two other men spoke. Sawyer and Cameron shouldn't have called Dylan; he had been through enough. He didn't need to be dragged back into this. But her younger brothers were impervious to her irritation, convinced that her resuming her undercover role was the wrong thing for her to do, and willing to go to any lengths to stop it.

"Can you guys clear out for a couple of minutes? I want to talk to Juliet alone," Dylan said after a few moments of silence.

Juliet picked up the handset as the three men filed out, her brothers grumbling under their breath. "Yeah, Dylan, they're gone."

"Listen, sis, here's the deal. You and Evan were a tight team once. He has always held to the opinion that you would one day resume duties as an active agent again. I know him, and he believes you can do this."

"It didn't sound that way a minute ago."

"It's not an easy case, Juliet, and you don't have much time to prepare. Plus you're still dealing with trauma and haven't been out there for over a year. Evan is just giving his honest opinion."

"Yeah, I know." And honestly, nobody knew even the half of what was going on with her. If they did, they sure wouldn't trust Juliet with their life.

"If it was anybody else but Evan you'd be going with, I'd tell you to refuse, no matter what. But he has always been…"

She waited for Dylan to finish his thought. "Always been what?"

"Nothing. Never mind. You should just know that he has your back. You can always trust that about Evan. He would die before he let anyone hurt you again."

"I don't know if I can do this, Dylan." The words came out as little more than a whisper. "What if I get both Evan and myself killed?"

"Jules, listen, you have good instincts. Follow those and trust them. And stay as close to him as you can."

Juliet's heart gave a little thump. The thought of being close to Evan was both thrilling and terrifying at the same time.

"But hey," Dylan continued, "I'm the first one on your side if you don't want to do this. I know Cady has the codes and I know it's bad. But it can be somebody else's job to get in there, some other way, and pull this off."

But Juliet knew that in the time it would take to come up with and implement a new plan, the codes would be sold and ultimately lives would be lost. And it would be her fault.

She took a deep breath. "No, I can do it, Dylan."

"I never doubted it for a second, sis."

They said their goodbyes and Juliet hung up. So this was it. She was going back undercover. Juliet walked toward the door. There was no point delaying; she needed all the time she could get before they were to meet with Cady in just a few days.

The guys weren't in the hallway, so she began walking to her office. There were a few things she needed to take care of before throwing herself into the Lisa Sinclair role.

Juliet was totally unprepared for the hands that grabbed her from behind as she walked. For the second time that day, her heart dropped into her stomach. For a moment she froze, terrified.

But then, unlike this morning, without a second thought she sprang into action. She rammed her elbow into the solar plexus behind her, and heard a whoosh of air release at her ear. The hands gripping her momentarily loosened, and she grabbed one of her attacker's arms and pulled it over her shoulder. Then she dropped her weight, widened her stance and flipped the person over her back. He was a large male, but weight didn't matter in this maneuver, just momentum.

Juliet was coming down with a punch to finish her attack when she realized she was looking into the face of her brother Cameron. Her dazed brother. She barely stopped her fist from connecting with his face.

"Cameron, what the hell are you doing?" Evan yelled.

Juliet stepped back and attempted to relax her arms at her sides, though it was difficult with the adrenaline rushing through her. Her fists were still clenched, ready to take on her attacker. Who happened to be her stupid brother.

"I was trying to prove a point," he finally said from where he lay on the floor, after getting his breath back.

Other people were coming out into the hallway to see what the commotion was about. But evidently a Branson brother lying on the floor wasn't much cause for concern, because most headed back the way they'd come without much real interest.

Sawyer reached down to help his brother up. "And what point was that?"

"That Juliet isn't ready. She can't stand to be touched. She's unpredictable."

Juliet could still feel tension coursing through her body. Fight or flight instincts, although neither were needed now.

Evan just shook his head. "I think all you successfully proved, you moron, is that your sister can kick your ass."

Cameron dusted off his clothes. "What is she going to do, flip everyone who touches her at Vince Cady's house?" He clenched his jaw, his exasperation clear.

"Well, then they'll learn pretty darn quickly not to touch her if they don't want to end up staring at the ceiling, wondering what the hell happened," Evan retorted.

"She's not ready, Evan," Cameron all but growled. "You're forcing her into something she doesn't want to do."

"I'm not forcing her into anything, Cam." Evan's rigid posture spoke volumes. "The situation sucks, I'm the first to admit it. But people are going to die if we don't get the drone codes out of Cady's hands, or whoever he plans to sell them to."

Juliet had had enough of this. All of it. "Why are you guys talking about me like I'm not even here?"

Cameron began to answer, but she cut him off. "You zip it. You lost your right to speak when you were lying on the floor. You're lucky I didn't break your nose."

Sawyer snickered. Juliet turned and pointed at him. "You be quiet, too. Just because you weren't stupid enough to try something so asinine doesn't mean you're off the hook."

Evan wisely made no sound at all.

"I know this situation isn't optimal. I know I'm not a good candidate for undercover work. Believe me, I've been thinking about that every day for the past eighteen months."

Both Cameron and Sawyer began to speak, but she held out her hand to stop them. "However, we don't have any other options that won't end up costing other people their lives. So I'm going to do it." She glanced at Evan. "And hopefully not get both of us killed in the process."

Evan nodded with a half smile, still smart enough to keep quiet.

"You two—" she waved at her brothers "—need to either get behind me on this or completely out of the way. No more trying to point out my shortcomings. I need your support."

With that, Juliet turned and walked down the hallway toward her office. She knew she didn't have to say anything more. Her brothers were hardheaded and often pretty stupid—Cameron's little stunt was plenty of proof of that—but she knew they loved her. And now that they understood she was serious about this, she knew they would stop their antics and help her and Evan in any way they could.

Juliet just hoped it would be enough.

Chapter Nine

Evan watched Juliet walk down the hall.

"All right. I guess this is really happening," Cameron muttered. "I didn't expect her to drop me like that."

"Yeah, she's in top shape. I saw her sparring yesterday. If anything, she's even more quick and strong than when she was an active agent," Evan said. It was damn impressive.

"But she's not consistent," Sawyer told him. "Yeah, she took Cameron down, but was just as likely to freeze up and do nothing."

"She'll get her rhythm back. She just needs more time to get used to being an agent again."

Sawyer slapped him on the back. "Well, unfortunately, that's the one thing you don't have—time."

Evan nodded. "Then I better not waste any more of it talking to you guys."

Sawyer stopped him. "Evan, you know we only said all that because we want to protect Juliet. I don't know if she'd survive another—" Sawyer lowered his voice "—incident. Like what happened before."

"Nothing like that's going to happen. I'll make sure of it." That was the one thing Evan knew he could promise.

"If she's made up her mind, then we want to help any

way we can," Cameron added. "We can clear our schedule, work with you for the next couple of days if you want."

Evan shook his head. He knew what needed to be worked on first and foremost with Juliet, and her brothers couldn't help. "Thanks, guys. I'll let you know if we need anything. Besides, she's pretty pissed at you two right now. I think you better steer clear."

"Yeah, the demonstration maybe wasn't such a great idea," Cameron mumbled.

"I could've told you that if you'd asked me beforehand, dumbass," Evan declared. "It's amazing you ever got your gorgeous fiancée to agree to marry someone as stupid as you."

"That's the truth," Sawyer said in agreement. "I never would've done something so dumb."

Evan didn't have much mercy for Sawyer, either, even though they'd been best friends since elementary school. "Yeah, I recall you saying some pretty stupid things to your own fiancée a few months ago, so you can't talk much either."

The Branson brothers began walking down the corridor, grumbling at each other about who was the most stupid when it came to women. Evan turned in the direction of Juliet's office. One thing was definitely true: they didn't have much time. They needed a crash course in working together, and it had to begin immediately.

Because if Lisa Sinclair jerked away every time her loving husband touched her—or flipped him over her shoulder—everyone in Cady's operation was going to get suspicious real fast.

She had to learn to let "Bob" touch her, to be around her. To kiss her.

Seeing that she had withdrawn from even the slightest

physical contact with anyone over the past year and a half, undoing it in a little over two days wasn't going to be easy.

Plus, Evan wanted to do some surveillance on Cady's house, at least the outer grounds, before they went in on Wednesday. The more they knew about the location, the better it would be.

Theoretically.

Evan tapped on Juliet's office door. "I come in peace."

She looked up from where she sat at her desk. "I know my brothers are your best friends, but they are really idiots sometimes."

"No argument here." Evan sat down in a nearby chair. "But if it helps, they're on board now. Anything you need or want for this op, just ask them and they'll get it to you."

Juliet nodded. "I know they're worried about me. I don't blame them."

"You're going to do fine." Looking at her now, so comfortable in her office, her color just slightly heightened from the fight with her brother, Evan believed his own words.

"I noticed when you were telling Dylan what happened that you left out the part where I hurled my guts all over the pavement. That's not exactly the most confidence-inspiring action."

Evan shrugged. "We've all lost it a time or two. Throwing up isn't the worst way someone's dealt with the stress of an op. Plus, you didn't do it while we were surrounded by Cady and his men. That's what counts."

"But what if I had, Evan?" Juliet's posture was hunched, her voice strained. "What if I had lost it right there in the middle of everything?"

"Then we would've dealt with it. Like anything that doesn't go your way while you're undercover. We would've blamed the guy who grabbed you, or the Avian flu, or told them you were pregnant. But we would've come up with something."

Juliet didn't look convinced.

"We can't prepare for every possibility in the field. That's why not everyone is cut out for working undercover. You have to think on your feet and be ready for anything."

"Yeah, well, I don't know that I'm able to do that anymore. I could barely think at all at the warehouse this morning."

"We'll stick together as much as possible, have each other's backs. And always, if you don't know what to say, the best bet is to say as little as possible."

Juliet's grin was wry. "That shouldn't be a problem for me."

"Are you nearly done here? I don't think we can afford to waste any time. We're going to need every bit of the days we have before meeting Cady."

She nodded. "Yeah. Burgamy all but jumped for joy when I told him I was going back undercover as Lisa Sinclair. Then got this very smug look on his face, like he knew it would happen all along. He had Chantelle clear everything off my plate for the next couple of weeks."

"Poor Chantelle. I don't know how she can bear being that close to Burgamy all the time."

Juliet began gathering up papers, straightening her desk. "I won't waste any more time around here, so you and I can get to work prepping for the op. And I won't be offended, Evan, if you feel we need to start back at the very beginning. As if I'm fresh out of the academy." But he could tell she found the thought distasteful.

"Even if you were straight out of the FBI Academy, you've still got good instincts, Jules. You're just going to need to learn not to panic. You've got the skills, we just have to hone them. It'll all come back."

Evan walked over to her desk and helped her collect and stack the files that had to do with Vince Cady. Juliet's discomfort grew as he got closer to her. Normally he would've backed off, given her the space she requested with her nonverbal communication. But not now.

Physical distance between the two of them was over. Their lives would depend on it.

Evan never actually touched her, but definitely came near enough to invade her personal space. Juliet didn't say anything, but shifted away, avoiding eye contact and rocking slightly.

That sort of behavior was more likely to get them killed while undercover than anything else. She couldn't cringe every time he was near.

"Jules." Evan kept his tone soft, even. "Lisa Sinclair wouldn't shy away from Bob. He's her husband. They love each other."

She nodded jerkily and stopped sliding farther away. But she was obviously still uncomfortable. Evan moved nearer.

"It's just me, Jules," he said softly into her ear. "I've been this close to you a hundred times before."

JULIET KNEW WHAT Evan said was true. They had been this close countless times before. She had known him since they were teenagers. He'd been running around with her brothers for almost as long as she could remember.

Evan was never going to hurt her.

Juliet tried to relax into that knowledge. The presence of such a large man—she came only up to his chin—so close beside her was still unsettling, but this was Evan. It was okay. Juliet took a deep breath and let the fear ease out of her system.

This is Evan. She repeated it in her head like a mantra.

They finished stacking the files. Evan helped her put them into her bag.

"So what's the plan?" Juliet asked him.

"When was the last time you fired your weapon?"

"I've kept current. Been at the range at least weekly."

"Good, because we don't have time to mess with that. We've got more important things to do, like go grocery shopping."

Of all the things Juliet could think of that needed to be done before their next meeting with Cady—memorization of her undercover role, brushing up on hand-to-hand combat, going over details about Cady and his known associates, coming up with a solid overall *plan*—none involved walking leisurely through a grocery store.

But that's where she found herself forty-five minutes later. Strolling through the local grocery store, pushing a cart, Evan right next to her helping her pick out produce.

As if they were on their fifth date and about to make a romantic meal together.

And the crazy thing was, for the first time in as long as Juliet could remember, the thought of a romantic meal didn't make her want to be sick to her stomach.

Evan didn't talk to her about the case or Vince Cady. He just talked about normal stuff, as if they were getting to know each other.

"Fresh strawberry pie is my favorite. Although apple pie with ice cream…I don't know that anything in the world is much better than that. How about you?"

Juliet stared at him as he handed her a pint of strawberries to put in their cart. His thumb grazed her hand as he did it. Juliet could swear she could feel where his thumb had touched her skin even after he moved away. "How about me, what?"

"What's your favorite kind of pie?" Evan took a small step closer and smiled at her.

That smile—the one that brought out the dimple in his chin—did something to Juliet's insides. Something she hadn't felt in a long time. Something she hadn't been sure she'd ever feel again.

The faintest stirrings of desire.

She immediately took a step back. "I don't know. I guess key lime pie is my favorite."

Yeah, Evan wanted her to be comfortable with him, but he didn't want her actually *wanting* him, she was sure. Plus, she totally couldn't think about feelings right now. Just surviving the next few days.

But she couldn't stop looking at the dimple in his chin.

Juliet tried to keep everything professional, yet friendly between them as they walked around the store. It was hard, given the way Evan constantly touched her, just briefly, or smiled, or said something funny to make her laugh.

Eventually they gathered all the food Evan deemed necessary for whatever meal he had planned, then paid and went out to his car. He had insisted she leave hers at Omega.

"Your house?" he asked her. "It's closest."

Juliet froze in the middle of putting a bag of groceries in the back of his Jeep. Evan couldn't see her house, not the state it was in right now. "No, let's go to your town house. That'll be better. Mine's a mess."

And she wasn't just talking about a mess, although it was a mess. She was talking about something else.

He didn't seem to have any argument with that, and Juliet relaxed. Evan just wouldn't understand what she'd done in her house. *Juliet* didn't even understand it.

Evan's town house wasn't too far from her place, just

a couple miles. They both lived north of DC, in College Park, a popular area for young professionals.

She had been to Evan's home a few years ago, but never just the two of them together. They pulled into his designated parking spot.

His home was different than Juliet remembered. Previously it had been more of a bachelor pad, with mismatched furniture, no color on the walls. She'd made fun of Evan and her brothers, about their poor taste in decorating, and the fact that some boxes remained unpacked in the middle of their living rooms. She had called all their places the bachelor death pads. They'd argued that they worked too much to be at home very often, anyway.

Now Evan's house couldn't be any more different. The walls were a deep teal, causing the white trim and molding to stand out brightly. The old couch and folding chairs in his living room had been replaced by a lovely overstuffed sofa and matching armchair, both of which fairly begged you to sit down, get comfortable and watch a movie with a loved one.

The room appealed to all Juliet's senses. She walked inside, looking around, amazed. "This is gorgeous. When did you do all this?"

Evan seemed uncomfortable, although Juliet had no idea why. "A little over a year ago. I thought it was finally time to grow up and stop looking like I was about to move out any second. I hired a decorator to help pick things out, although I did most of the work myself."

"Well, it's unbelievable." She spun away from him to look at the couch. "I couldn't have picked out a better color myself. And this sofa? I just want to sink into it and stay there forever."

Juliet knew she was gushing, but couldn't help it. She

loved everything about this room. Smiling widely, she turned back to Evan.

Only to find him looking at her with something akin to agony in his eyes.

"Evan? What's wrong?" She rushed to his side. "Are you okay?"

"Fine. Let's get this stuff into the kitchen." He blinked and his easy smile slid back into place. Juliet wondered if she had imagined the whole thing.

The kitchen was just as tastefully decorated as the living room. Evan now had matching appliances and granite countertops. An island rested in the middle of the space, two stools slid neatly underneath.

"Wow, whoever your decorator was, I want to kiss him or her."

"Her. Kimberly's pretty brilliant."

Juliet could hear the admiration Evan had for this woman. Had they been lovers? All of a sudden Juliet wasn't as enthralled with the colors and textures as she had been a moment ago.

Were they still lovers now? Juliet had avoided any personal conversations with Evan for a long time. She realized she had no idea what was going on in his life. For all she knew he could be seriously involved with someone. The thought that she was standing here, leaning against some other woman's kitchen island, did not sit well with her.

Juliet knew she had no claim on Evan, no say about his intimacy with other women. Because what could she do? It wasn't as if she could get involved with him, even if he wasn't dating someone. Men tended not to like it when their woman shied away from them every time they were touched.

So what did it matter if Evan had a gorgeous interior decorating girlfriend? If the woman didn't care if Evan went undercover as someone else's husband, then it was none of Juliet's business.

"Does, uh…Kimberly mind you going undercover for long periods?"

Evan looked up from where he was putting the fruits and vegetables into the refrigerator. "We're not dating. As a matter of fact, I think you might be more her type than I am."

Juliet just nodded, ignoring the fact that she suddenly loved everything about the town house again.

"Oh. Well, she did a great job in decorating. I love it here. Definitely not a bachelor death pad any longer."

Evan stopped and looked at her for a long moment.

"What?" Juliet finally asked.

"Nothing," he said. "Get over here and let's cook dinner."

Chapter Ten

All through the evening, as they cooked, ate and washed dishes, Evan tried to touch Juliet as much as he could. He stayed as close to her as possible, invading her space, even bumping her leg with his under the kitchen island as they ate dinner together.

She often shied away or flinched, and while something in Evan's soul shattered each time he saw those little reflexive reactions, he never brought it up. Talking about them wouldn't do any good.

It was time to change Juliet's basic muscle memory. Words weren't going to get her any more comfortable with being around him. Only being around him would do that.

Not that it was any hardship for Evan, being this close to Juliet. If he'd had his way he would've been this close to Juliet long before now. And would still be long after the case closed.

Yeah, this was forced intimacy rushed along for the sake of working undercover together. But Evan didn't mind at all. As a matter of fact, the closeness, the flirtation, just having her around felt totally right to him.

And her scent. Something about the smell of her hair—not fancy, just clean and fresh—made Evan want to keep her with him for about the next fifty years.

When she had commented on the decor and furniture

changes he'd made in his house, Evan had come to an abrupt realization. All of it had been for her. Not consciously. He'd never once thought *oh, Juliet will like this* while he'd worked with Kimberly, picking out colors and furniture a year ago.

But now, having Juliet here, seeing how much she genuinely liked what he'd done with the place, he realized it had all been for her. He had wanted her to have a place where she felt comfortable. Where she felt safe.

His subconscious hadn't had any grander plans than that. He hadn't been thinking she might move in and live here. He'd just wanted it to be a place where she could visit, and not think of it as a bachelor death pad.

He hadn't been sure when she might ever come here. He'd just wanted to have it ready whenever she finally did.

Now they were sitting side by side on the couch in his newly decorated living room, looking over files from the case. Juliet reached for another folder, then kicked one shoe off and tucked her foot beneath her when she sat back down. That caused her to slide a little closer to him. But she didn't move away, almost didn't seem to notice the proximity.

Evan smiled to himself. Maybe there was hope for this plan, after all.

"I've been studying Cady and everything we know about him for the past two days," she said. "He's a slippery bastard—has his fingers into everything. But honestly, I'm not sure his son, Christopher, isn't going to be more of a problem."

"Christopher? I don't know much about him. He's in his early twenties, right?"

"Yes, and is just starting to become an important part of his father's business."

"Why now?"

"We're not exactly sure. Intel suggests that he's been back in Vince's organization for only the last year."

"Where was he before that?" Evan asked.

Juliet reached forward and threw the very thin file Omega had on Christopher Cady onto the table. When she sat back, she moved farther away from Evan, leaning on the arm of the couch. "No one knows. We can't get any official word or record. But evidently, he hasn't been living in his parents' house since he was seventeen."

"But he's involved with his dad now?"

"Yes, for sure. Although he wasn't at the warehouse today."

"Hmm." Evan reached over and gently clasped the foot Juliet had tucked under her, drawing it onto his lap. He didn't want to give her a chance to begin withdrawing.

She looked at him sharply, then down at her foot, but didn't move away. "Word is that Christopher was in Europe. Cady has family over there. But nobody knows why he was living there instead of here."

Her eyelids began to close almost automatically when Evan started rubbing her foot through her thin sock. He found a knot of tension in the arch and applied pressure there with his thumb. She let out a soft little moan.

"What are you doing?" Juliet asked. But Evan noticed she didn't pull her foot away.

"Just trying to get some of the tension out of your system, so you can think clearly. It's been a pretty stressful day for you."

"But—"

"No buts, Jules. Just relax. And hand me your other foot while you're at it."

Evan just kept rubbing her instep as Juliet thought it through. He could almost see the emotions play out on her face: pleasure, confusion, even consternation. But no real fear. Eventually, the pleasure won out. She kicked off her other shoe and stretched that foot out, too, then leaned back into the arm of the couch as he worked his magic. Her eyes drifted shut.

"It's okay to go to sleep. Like I said, you've had a hard day."

"No, I'm not going to sleep. But I'll just rest here for a little while," Juliet murmured.

Evan loved how she burrowed back into the cushions just a little. He kept firmly rubbing her feet and ankles, easing tension out as best he could.

Slowly, her legs became heavier in his hands as she let go of more and more of her control. Despite her protests she was falling asleep. Good, she needed it. It was late; they'd both had an exhausting day. Plus they had even more to do over the next forty-eight hours, including scoping out as much as they could of the Cady residence before going there for the auction.

Evan debated about whether to carry Juliet upstairs to his bed, but decided against it. She'd probably wake up when he tried to move her, and demand to go home. He didn't want to let her out of his sight, or touch, for as many hours as possible. He wanted her subconscious to become used to him being around.

And hell, he could admit it, at least to himself, that he wanted everything about Juliet to become used to him being there, not just her subconscious.

Evan gently shifted her feet off his lap. He got up and turned off the lights, except for the hallway one, which he left on so Juliet wouldn't feel disoriented if she woke in the middle of the night. He walked back over to the couch and looked down at her sleeping form. No fear or worry seemed to surround her now. She had rolled onto her side and tucked one arm under her head.

Evan removed his shoes, then eased himself into the space between her and the back cushions of the couch. She stirred but didn't wake up.

Evan longed to pull her against him, but knew she might feel restrained if she woke up with arms around her. But he had to put his arm somewhere, so rested it on her hip. Juliet relaxed back against him and Evan fell asleep thinking he'd rather be on this cramped couch with her than alone on the largest, most comfortable bed.

JULIET WOKE UP with a start, unsure where she was. Not in her own home, that much she knew with certainty. Her back wasn't against the corner wall where she always slept in her house. Was she in her office?

Juliet wasn't in a panic. Odd. She couldn't remember the last time she'd woken up and wasn't in at least a little panic.

It didn't take long to remember where she was. Evan's house. In his wonderfully decorated living room, on his cozy couch.

And, based on the arm flung over her hip, Evan lay on the cozy couch with her.

Juliet waited in the dark for the fear to come. In the nest she had made for herself at home, the fear always came, stealing away any chance of falling back to sleep. Four or five hours of sleep had become the norm, although often she was able to take a nap on the sofa in her office.

But the fear wasn't coming now. Juliet relaxed slightly against Evan's sleeping form.

From where she lay, she could just see the window at the front of his town house. The sun was beginning to creep up. With a sense of shock, Juliet realized she had slept the entire night, not waking up once.

No nightmares. No screaming. No fighting nonexistent monsters in the darkness.

She shifted so she was lying on her back and could see Evan a little better in the dim light. He looked so relaxed and peaceful in his sleep. His brown hair fell slightly over his forehead. The growth on his cheeks was hours past a five o'clock shadow.

That tiny dimple was still there on his chin.

Juliet was amazed at how good it felt to just lie here. How right it felt. She wanted to stay here forever.

Beautiful hazel eyes slowly blinked open and looked at her. The smile that followed caused her heart to skip a beat.

"Hi," Evan murmured, his voice deep with sleep.

Juliet just stared at him for a long moment. Evan had been a source of strength for so long, a good friend, but always something more than that. And here she was, lying in his arms, fear nowhere to be found.

She was so very tired of being afraid.

Juliet closed the small distance between their bodies and kissed him. She didn't let herself think about it, just let herself feel.

Then Evan kissed her back and all she could do was feel. He teased her lips apart and drew her closer, rolling onto his back so she was half lying on top of him. She felt one of his hands on her waist, the other cupping her neck to keep her close.

Juliet remembered their kiss in front of the lighthouse, how intense it had been. But she didn't remember this heat, this electricity, running through her. She just wanted to get closer to Evan, and stay here forever.

But after a long moment he eased back, then sat up, bringing her with him.

"Wow," he murmured. He kept an arm around her and smiled at her tenderly.

"Yeah, wow," Juliet echoed. But she didn't want to talk about how good the kiss was, she just wanted to kiss some more. She started to reach for him again, but stopped at his words.

"That sort of thing ought to definitely convince Vince Cady and his group that we're happily married."

Her arm froze in midair, then dropped back to her side.

This was all just undercover practice for Evan, of course. Duh.

That hadn't been a real kiss for him, and especially hadn't been real emotion. It had just been practice for the roles they were playing. The heat had obviously been only one-sided.

"Yep." Juliet popped the *p*, trying to sound casual. She slid away from him on the couch. "We're definitely getting closer to being ready."

He pulled her back. "You're doing great, Jules." She could feel him kiss the side of her head. "It's all going to work."

Juliet thought of the drone override codes Cady planned to sell, and the damage those could do. Yeah, Evan was right to keep his focus on the job at hand. She needed to do the same.

And she needed to remember that nothing Evan did, despite how good it might make her feel, was real in any way. He wasn't attracted to her; this was the job.

Juliet's phone buzzed from the coffee table. She picked it up, cringing as she saw the screen. Lisa Sinclair had received another email.

Sweetheart, I'm so worried about you. You should be mine, no one else's. We'll be together soon.

Chapter Eleven

Evan watched as Juliet all but threw her phone across the table. She jumped off the couch as if it had burned her and walked over to the window.

"Everything okay? What happened?"

"Nothing. It's fine. Nothing."

She was looking out the window, rubbing a fist against her stomach as if something inside hurt. And she wasn't just glancing out, she seemed to be looking for something or someone in particular.

Evan reached over and grabbed her phone to see if it held clues, but there was nothing on the screen.

He joined her at the window. The reflection showed her pinched expression. "It's obviously not nothing, Juliet. Are you looking for someone?" He peered out the window himself, but there was no one to be seen in the early dawn. The streets were empty.

Evan touched Juliet's shoulders, wanting to let her know that she wasn't alone in whatever was upsetting her, but she jerked away.

Damn it, were they back to square one?

He reached out again to rub her arm, but she shrugged him off and walked back to the couch.

"What's going on, Juliet? Seriously."

She shook her head. "Nothing. I don't want to talk about it."

His jaw clenched. "That's the problem, isn't it? You never want to talk about it. Never want to talk about anything, to let any of us in."

Juliet didn't respond, just walked over to the gym bag she'd brought from the office. "I'm not ready to talk about stuff yet." Her voice was soft as she rifled through the bag. She pulled out running shorts and a top, not looking at him. "I don't know if I'm ready for any of this, Evan."

He rubbed a weary hand across his forehead. He didn't want to push, didn't want to lose all the progress that they'd made over the past few hours. And that kiss a few minutes ago—Evan couldn't even allow himself to think about that right now. He'd have to process it later.

"Okay, let's go for a run. Together. No talking necessary," he told her.

He thought she might refuse, but then she nodded. "Okay."

They were out the door just a few minutes later, headed toward a local park. Juliet had no problem keeping up with the pace Evan set, even given her shorter stride, further testament of what good shape she'd kept herself in. Her brain might not quite be ready for her to resume an active agent position, but the same couldn't be said for her body.

They jogged around and through the park without talking, Juliet obviously not interested in sharing what was on her mind. Evan wished he could tell her that no matter how fast or how far she ran, the demons she tried to leave behind would still be there when she stopped. You couldn't outrun your demons.

You had to face them. Maybe it was time to help her do that.

They reached a large fountain in the middle of the park

and Evan stopped, rather abruptly. Juliet looked over at him in concern. "Are you okay?"

"Yes," he told her between breaths. They were both sweating and breathing hard. They had kept up a strong pace for at least five or six miles. "I want you to close your eyes."

"Why?"

"Just do it, okay, Jules? For me."

Juliet shook her head, but closed her eyes as he asked.

Evan looked around the park, now much more active, since it wasn't so early.

"Okay, without looking, I want you to tell me what's going on around here."

"What?" Juliet's tone was uncertain, her eyebrows squished together over her closed eyes.

"What's happening in this park right now? If you had to describe it to someone, what would you say?"

Juliet shook her head, obviously thinking he had lost it, but took a deep breath through her nose and blew it out of her mouth.

"A mother with two toddlers at the southwest corner, heading toward the playground. Another woman with a stroller coming in from the other direction. Male Caucasian runner, age thirty-five to forty-five, dark hair, six foot one, 170 pounds, running counterclockwise on the inner loop. Blonde female speed walking with German shepherd on inner loop, probably five foot three, 150 pounds. African-American couple, early twenties, strolling together five hundred yards from the fountain. Drinking coffee from nearby coffeehouse—"

"That's fine." Evan chuckled. "You can open your eyes. I think you proved my point."

"And what the heck was that?" Juliet asked as she

opened her eyes and looked around, obviously checking to see what she had missed.

Which was nothing.

"Your brain saw and processed everything, Jules. Even though you were running at a hard pace and there was no reason to keep track of what was going on, your brain still did it automatically."

"So?"

"So? Your body still works like an agent and so does your mind. Your situational awareness is off the charts. Only your fears are holding you back." Evan prayed he wasn't pushing her further away from him. "I'm not saying you should just get over what happened. I'm just saying I think you can move forward."

Juliet looked around the park again, then stared at him for a long time. At first he thought she was going to argue, but she didn't. She looked down at the phone she held in her hand, then back up at him, her expression resolved.

"Okay, Evan, you want the truth about my fears? We're not far from my house. Let's go there."

EVAN WASN'T SURE what her house had to do with her fears, but jogged the mile or so to her place, slowing down and walking the last few blocks with her. He hadn't been here since the attack, although he had hung out here all the time with her brothers before that.

Juliet hadn't wanted to go to any of their bachelor death pads, so she'd had them over to her place when they wanted to eat or hang out or watch a movie. Her space was smaller, but it was always clean and inviting, and most importantly, usually had real food.

As Juliet let Evan in, using a key she had kept in her running belt, shock reverberated through him. Even from just inside the door, he couldn't believe this was the same place. He blinked rapidly as if the scene before him might change to what it was supposed to be—a light, airy, friendly house.

Not the hovel that stood before him.

The chic wooden blinds that used to cover the windows had been replaced by heavy curtains that obviously hadn't been opened in months. Barely any illumination from the sun made it through, casting the entire place in an eerie light. Every flat surface was piled with papers and files and *stuff*, not to mention layers of dust. There was nowhere to sit even if you wanted to.

Obviously, Juliet hadn't done any entertaining in her house recently. It looked as if she hadn't even been here herself. Had she moved somewhere else and left her furniture behind?

But when Evan turned and looked into the kitchen, which was located across the small foyer from her living room, he realized that wasn't the case. The kitchen was in slightly better shape. No food was left out, and dishes were washed and sitting on the drying rack, but there were newspapers and books stacked on the small table. Obviously, she did use this kitchen, but evidently ate while standing at the counter.

Evan scrambled to understand what he was seeing. Juliet said nothing and closed the door they'd just walked through. And then began locking the most locks Evan had ever seen at a single entrance.

There were at least a half dozen that bolted her door into the wall. He watched with an aching chest as she rapidly clicked each lock into place—a testament of how often she did it.

Yes, Juliet did live here, in this house, in its current state. But you couldn't call it her home. You couldn't have called this *anybody's* home.

Juliet still didn't speak, just walked into the kitchen and grabbed a water bottle for each of them, then headed down the hall into one of the two bedrooms. Not hers, but the room she'd made into her home office.

This room was obviously used often. Her desk, complete with lamp and computer, was like her office at Omega: meticulous and clean, the exact opposite state of her living room. No dust, no piles of junk. At the other end was a small couch, a pillow and blanket thrown over it.

Juliet pointed to the couch. "I sleep there every once in a while."

Evan supposed that sleeping some nights on a couch might not be unusual for a person who had been through what she had. Heaven knew, he had his own nightmares about that day. He imagined Juliet's were much worse, since she had lived through it.

"Nobody can blame you for having bad nights, Jules. Sleeping on the couch every once in a while happens to everyone."

She studied him for a moment, then crossed into her master bedroom, motioning for him to follow. There were heavy drapes over the window in here, also, allowing in very little light. Her queen-size bed, with its beautiful four posters—Evan remembered how delighted Juliet had been when she'd found it at a secondhand store about five years ago—obviously hadn't been slept in for months, maybe longer. Like the kitchen table and furniture in the living room, it was covered with stuff: jackets, boxes, papers.

But Evan was totally unprepared when Juliet pulled open the door to her walk-in closet and pointed down at the floor—to a makeshift bed of a couple blankets and a pillow. Next to it lay a rifle—a .308 Winchester, it looked like—and a Glock G42, similar to the handgun Juliet used as an agent.

"That's where I sleep—*attempt* to sleep—almost all the time. I haven't slept in a bed since the attack."

She turned and walked out of the closet and her bedroom. Evan remained, staring at the pitiful pallet that spoke volumes about Juliet's solitude and fear.

He'd had no idea. None of them had known Juliet was struggling to such a degree. All of them knew she spent a lot of time at work and hadn't been home much. Looking around now, Evan could see why. No one would want to spend much time here. And obviously, a lot of the time she spent here was in fear.

Evan's heart broke just thinking about it. But anger wasn't far behind.

He followed her into the kitchen, where she leaned against the sink.

"So, obviously, I'm not fit for duty. You know I've been talking to therapists for months, all different types, but never seem to mention this." Juliet laughed nervously and gestured with her hand. "This is barely a step up from that reality show about hoarding. Criminals probably wish I would become an agent again, because obviously, I'm damaged beyond—"

Evan pulled her into his arms. He didn't care if the movement might startle her or make her tense. He just wanted her to know she wasn't alone. Not anymore.

By God, never again would she have to go through any of this alone. If she wasn't getting better, then Evan, not to mention her brothers, would help her. In any way she needed, whatever way she needed.

"Jules, why didn't you tell us?" Evan whispered against her hair, glad that she didn't try to pull away. "We all knew you didn't like to be touched, but none of us knew you were struggling so much here at home." Evan couldn't wrap his head around it.

"I didn't know what to say."

"None of us expect you to just get over what happened, but hasn't it gotten any better at all? This place..." Evan glanced into the living room. "It's like you're waiting for another attack."

"That's what I feel like whenever I'm here. Like I'm not safe." Juliet removed herself from his arms and pointed at the locks. "Although it would seem impossible with all that."

"Jules, why are you still so afraid? The man who attacked and raped you is dead. His accomplice is in federal prison. Neither of them can hurt you anymore."

"Somebody is still out there, Evan."

Evan ran a weary hand over his forehead and eyes. This was so much worse than he'd thought. If Juliet was still this scared after eighteen months, and thought someone was after her, then the psychological scarring must be much deeper. She was definitely not ready to go back undercover. He would need to cancel the mission and find another way to get the drone codes from Cady.

Because honestly, Evan was worried for Juliet's very sanity.

How had he not seen this? How had they all been so blind to what Juliet was really going through? She should have been getting better, not worse. And now, thinking someone was after her when it was impossible...

Evan walked toward where she stood in the middle of the room, moving slowly, as if she were a wild animal he didn't want to spook. "Juliet, there's nobody who can hurt you anymore. There hasn't been since the arrest. You don't need to be afraid of that."

She looked torn between wanting to accept his embrace and argue the point further, but then froze when her phone chirped. The same sound it had made this morning.

Evan watched all the color leak from Juliet's face as she stared at the device.

"That's the reason I know someone is still out there, still after me. He's been sending me—well, Lisa Sinclair—messages for nearly a year."

Chapter Twelve

Evan pulled Juliet to his side—she had her fist clutched against her stomach again—and grabbed the phone. It was a link to an email she'd received as Lisa Sinclair, and that had been forwarded to her phone.

Are you thinking about me as much as I'm thinking about you? It's so hard for us to be apart, isn't it? Soon, sweetheart.

There was no signature line or name. Nothing to give away the identity of the sender.

The questions flew through Evan's mind almost faster than he could ask them. "Juliet, what the hell is this? How long has it been happening? Why didn't you tell anybody about it?"

Juliet shrugged. "I was trying to handle it myself. I don't know who it's from—and believe me, I've tried every resource Omega has to figure that out. It's someone with advanced hacking and cloaking skills sending those messages."

"How many have there been?"

"Dozens. Escalating in the past few months. Here, I'll show you." She led him back to the room that contained her computer.

Juliet opened the file with the emails and got up from the chair so Evan could sit there. Rage pooled in his stomach as he read.

It's hard to be alone, isn't it? Soon we'll be together, sweetheart.

I'd never let anything so horrible happen to you. Don't worry sweetheart, I know you'll want me.

I'm much better for you than that no-good husband of yours, sweetheart. We'll get rid of him so we can be together.

The only tears I'd ever make you cry are ones of pleasure, sweetheart.

Don't worry, sweetheart. When we're together you'll never think of your past again.

Soon, sweetheart, soon. Be patient. I'm coming for you.

Thirty or so more, all like that. All with the same sick use of the word *sweetheart*, and many with intimate, graphic descriptions of Juliet's rape a year and a half ago. The blood pounded in Evan's ears, his desire to put a fist through the closest wall almost overwhelming.

He closed his eyes, tried to focus on the task at hand.

"They're all addressed to Lisa Sinclair, with no link to you or anything with Omega?" He spun the chair around to face Juliet.

She sat on the couch, clutching the pillow to her chest. "No. I don't think it's someone who knew Lisa Sinclair was just my undercover persona. It's someone who thinks she's real. That I'm really her."

Evan leaned back in the chair. "Have you had any indication of anyone following you? Is it possible that your association with Omega has been compromised?"

"No, I've never seen anyone. And believe me, I've

looked. I don't think it's someone who knows me as Juliet Branson, but..."

"But it's someone who has details he shouldn't have about your attack," Evan finished.

Juliet nodded.

She had never made the extent of her attack public knowledge at Omega. All details had been struck from her file. Most people knew she had been hurt—she'd been in the hospital too long for that to go unnoticed—but none of them would have the sick details present in these emails.

"It has to be someone who was there." Juliet's voice was barely more than a whisper.

The Avilo brothers had taken her in the middle of the night, while she was sleeping. Knocked her unconscious, then dragged her out to the nearby boat shed. Evan and Juliet had been undercover as Bob and Lisa, staying at a local weapons dealer's mansion, for buys that were occurring all weekend. There had been multiple third parties around, including the buyers who had become so upset at Bob and Lisa's success.

Evan had been playing poker with the men, trying to wring any information he could from them, and Juliet had been back in their locked room alone.

A single lock hadn't kept out her attackers, which probably explained her need for a half dozen on her door now.

When Evan had gotten back to their room and found it empty, he had immediately begun looking for her. Juliet would not have left it in the middle of the night without giving him any notification, unless it was under duress.

It was under the worst possible duress.

Finding her haunted Evan's dreams even now. She'd been mostly naked and tied to a post, with a broken leg, cracked ribs from brutal kicks, covered in bruises and blood. Moaning, barely coherent.

Both her eyes had been swollen shut from punches, and she hadn't known it was Evan when he'd first approached her. She had tried to scream, but it had come out a broken croak, barely audible.

Evan had reassured her the best he could, untied her and wrapped her in his shirt, screaming for an ambulance. At that moment, he couldn't have cared less that they were undercover. He'd just wanted Juliet to get the medical attention she needed. Although no one had figured out they were undercover, anyway.

Juliet had been too traumatized to talk then, but two days later, when he found out the extent of what had happened, and who was responsible—Robert and Marco Avilo—Evan had made sure they had gone down. One was dead, the other in prison.

But had he missed someone?

"Was a third person there that night, Juliet?" Evan asked in the gentlest tone he could muster. He knew she didn't like talking about it.

"No. I've gone over it in my head, believe me. The Avilo brothers were only the two people involved. One who held me down and the other—" Juliet put the pillow aside and stood up.

"The messages started almost a year ago. Honestly, at first I didn't know what to think. Maybe that it was some twisted joke from someone inside Omega. And then…" Juliet was pacing now.

"And then what?" Evan finally asked.

"Remember when I took those personal days about ten months ago?"

He nodded. They'd all been relieved that she was going to spend a few days down in Florida with some girlfriends at the beach. It had seemed a step in the direction of healing.

"Well, actually, I went down to the federal penitentiary in Louisiana to talk to the warden."

Evan instantly put together what she saying. "You went to see if Robert Avilo, the surviving brother, was the one sending you the emails."

Juliet stopped her pacing. "Robert Avilo wasn't the one who actually raped me, but he was there. He has the knowledge of the sick stuff in those emails. I had to know if it was him, Evan."

Evan didn't blame her. "What did you find out?"

"That it couldn't have been him. That he had no access to any computers, nor had he sent or received any correspondence since he'd been in prison. Evidently, his brother Marco was the only family he had."

"Robert didn't strike me as someone who could've hacked an IP address, anyway. Marco always seemed to be the brains of their little ring. Robert took orders from Marco."

Evan could see Juliet grinding her teeth from where he sat. She sank back down on the couch. "That was my thought, too." She shook her head. "I know you told me Marco had been killed while resisting arrest, and I wanted that to be true with every fiber of my being."

"But?" Evan could hear the *but* as clear as day.

"But I had to be sure."

He was afraid he knew where she was going with this. His shoulders slumped. "What did you do, Juliet?"

"I got a court order and had the body exhumed. I checked it for DNA."

"And?"

"And it was Marco Avilo. You were right. He had died of a bullet wound taken after he resisted arrest and shot at some officers."

Juliet shrugged. "So that left me back at ground zero.

Marco was dead and Robert had no access to any computer or any visitors. I just thought if I ignored the emails long enough, whoever was sending them would give up. I never responded. But it's gotten so much worse in the last three months. There have been so many more emails." She looked around as if seeing the shambles her house was in for the first time. "I should've said something."

Evan couldn't stand to hear the smallness of Juliet's voice. She shouldn't have tried to go through this alone, but she had nothing to be ashamed of.

He went to sit next to her on the couch, then picked her up and settled her on his lap, his arms around her. She drew in a startled breath, but didn't pull away.

"Yes, you should've said something." Evan put his lips against her temple. "But because this threat is real and anyone in this situation would need support, not because you're weak."

"I didn't want to bother anyone. You all had your own cases, your own problems. I didn't want to be a burden."

Evan didn't know whether to shake her or never let her out of his arms again. "Nothing about you could ever be a burden to me, Jules."

"I was afraid I was losing my mind." Juliet actually cuddled in closer to him. "Look at this place, Evan. It's not healthy. I knew that, but I couldn't seem to do anything about it."

"Well, you don't have to try to go through any of this alone anymore. That's the first step." He rubbed small circles on her back. "And we need to get some more people working on this email issue. Omega takes stalking seriously, regardless of the circumstances."

Juliet nodded. "I know. But once we tell Sawyer, Cam and Dylan, they're going to go crazy with the overprotectiveness. They're bad enough as it is."

Reluctantly, Evan shifted her from his lap. "Yeah, I should call them right now. We can let them know about this while we start working on a different plan for the case with Cady."

"Why do we need a different plan for Cady?"

"Juliet," Evan said softly, gently. "I was wrong to force you to go back undercover. You don't have to do it. We'll find another way."

She shot off the couch, turned and glared at him. "You didn't *force* me to go back under, Evan. I agreed to do it because it was the right thing, and because if those drone codes get out there, a lot of people are going to die."

Evan looked around at the shambles of her house. "Jules—"

"Okay, I'll admit I've been having problems. Here, alone at night, my demons come out and obviously I haven't been terribly successful at battling them. But that doesn't change the situation with Cady. Bob and Lisa Sinclair *as a couple* is the only good option for getting the codes out before they're sold to someone else on the black market."

What Juliet said was true, but the thought of doing any further damage to her psyche tore at Evan. He wanted to protect her more than anything else.

Juliet was looking at him with something akin to pleading in her eyes. "Evan, is what you said in the park today true? Do you really feel like I have it in me to be a successful agent, to get the job done at Cady's?"

Was he making her beg to do something she didn't even really want to do?

"Juliet, wait—"

"Because I don't want to get either of us hurt or killed. And I'm scared. But I'm more scared of the drones being used on innocent people. I couldn't live with myself if I had a chance to stop it, but was too much of a coward."

Evan couldn't take any more. He rose and went to her. He gripped her biceps gently, running his thumbs along the smooth skin of her arms. "Yes, I believe all those things I said. Nothing has changed that—even though you're now the one with the bachelor death pad."

Evan kissed her softly, briefly. But he knew this wasn't the time for anything more, so he pulled away. "You can do anything you set your mind to. I've never doubted that for a moment."

"I'm afraid I'll screw up."

"I'm afraid I'll screw up, too. But we won't. We'll just work together and do what we do best," Evan said with a wink. "Catch some bad guys and save the world."

Chapter Thirteen

Something released inside Juliet. A weight lifted off her shoulders now that the truth about the sweetheart emails, as they decided to call them, was out in the open. They took her computer to Omega to be examined. She explained to Evan that she'd tried using Omega resources before, but agreed the sheer volume of emails she'd received over the past few weeks warranted a second look. Maybe there'd be some clue about who was sending them.

Evan also helped Juliet make a dent in cleaning up her house. It wasn't actually dirty—she hadn't left food out or anything that had attracted any sort of bugs, and none of it was garbage. Instead, the clutter consisted mostly of old reports, files, books, maps, mail.

Almost as if her subconscious had attempted to build a fortress of paper around her.

When Evan opened the drapes covering her windows, Juliet watched, blinking rapidly as her eyes attempted to adjust. It had been months since this much light had been let into this house. Letting light in being a fitting metaphor.

They didn't spend all day in the house, knowing there was too much other pressing business from the case. Juliet packed a bag so she could stay at Evan's place for a few days. It would be better, just in case they were ever followed, if they seemed to live in the same house.

Juliet knew that tomorrow they would need to move into full agent mode, including infiltrating and scoping out Cady's house as much as possible tomorrow night. Any information they had before going in on Wednesday would only help them. Plus it would give Juliet a chance to reacclimate herself with clandestine incursion tactics.

Surprisingly, she felt equal parts ready and scared to death.

Dinner was nice, just the two of them at Evan's town house. But afterward, while discussing the case and the details of Vince Cady's residence, Juliet heard the dreaded chirp from her phone, the sound she had assigned to signify the receipt of another sweetheart email.

She didn't realize how relaxed she'd become in Evan's presence until the tension flooded back through her.

This was the third email she'd received that day. The frequency of the messages was definitely escalating, particularly today.

"You okay?" he asked, reaching for her hand.

"I won't lie, I don't like getting these. And three in one day?" She chewed at her bottom lip, but then forced herself to stop. "But I'm glad you know, Evan." She grasped his outstretched hand. Even through the fear she could feel little sparks of attraction where their palms touched. She wondered if it was the same for him.

"I'm glad you don't have to go through this alone anymore. Nobody should have to." Evan squeezed her hand.

"I just hope receiving these emails won't interfere with the case. I don't want to just ignore them in case the perp slips up and says something useful that'll help us catch him."

Evan nodded. "How about if we look at them together from now on when you get one. Keep everything in perspective and on an even keel."

"That would be great." Juliet kissed him on the cheek. "Thank you, Evan. I know today hasn't been easy on you, either."

"We'll just take it as it comes. But no more hiding stuff."

"Deal." She smiled, and for the first time in a long while, it wasn't forced.

Evan stood. "I'm going to go shower and get ready for bed. I left a towel and stuff out for you in the guest bathroom."

"Okay, thanks."

He turned as he was heading out of the living room. "And Jules, I was thinking…" He seemed uncharacteristically at a loss for words. "At your house you showed me the couch and the pallet in the closet where you said you've slept since the attack. That you haven't been back in a bed?"

Juliet sighed inwardly. It must have seemed ludicrous to him, her blankets on the closet floor. "Do you think I'm crazy?"

"Not at all." His smile was gentle. "You did what you had to do to get by. Nobody would think that's crazy. But once we get to Vince Cady's house, you can't sleep on the floor."

She hadn't really thought of that. "Right, yeah."

"And we'll probably be under surveillance, so I wanted to address that now. You can't be all tense and nervous getting into bed with me there."

"Right, yeah." Juliet felt like a parrot.

"So, it would probably be a good idea for both of us to sleep together in my bed tonight. So you're more used to being in a bed…"

"And being with *you* in a bed."

Evan grinned. "I promise to stay on my side, if that's any consolation."

The thing was, Juliet wasn't sure if it was or not. And she wondered what Evan would do if she told him that.

She needed to remember that this intimacy, the heat she could feel between them, was just because of his undercover skills, not because of any real attraction. At least on his part.

But she'd like to see some more of his "undercover" skills.

The thought popped into her head before she could stop it. Shocked, Juliet brought both hands up to cover her mouth, just in case the words came shooting out. And she giggled.

She didn't know who was more surprised by the sound, Evan or her.

"What's going on in that head of yours?" he asked, still grinning.

"Nothing." Juliet tried to pull herself together. "Got it. Bed, together, for the case. No problem. I'm going to take a shower, too. Um, in the guest shower, I mean. I'll see you in a few minutes."

She was still snickering as she fled the scene of the crime.

Undercover.

SHAKING HIS HEAD, Evan watched Juliet all but run down the hallway. What the heck had just happened? He had no idea.

But if it made her smile and giggle like that, he'd take it no matter what it was.

Since the information about the sweetheart emails had come to light, Juliet had been more relaxed, freer, than Evan could remember seeing her since the attack. And she didn't cringe from his touch. At least not as much. And sometimes even initiated a touch herself.

Evan found it difficult to believe how happy it made him

when Juliet touched him of her own accord. Even something as simple as a brush of her hand on his arm meant more to him than entire embraces from other women.

He was feeling better about this operation than he had since Juliet showed up at the warehouse yesterday morning. He'd lost faith for a little while when he'd seen the state of her house, but now, understanding the reason, he could even understand that.

And she had just giggled and run out of the room.

And they were about to sleep together in his bed.

The thought of it thrilled Evan in ways he never would have thought. And it wasn't about sex. Obviously, Juliet wasn't agreeing to have sex with him, so he could just push that thought right out of his mind. Which, surprisingly, didn't upset him one bit.

Just the thought of being in bed next to her was more than enough. Able to help her if she needed him, or just knowing she was sleeping peacefully even if he didn't.

In the dark, lying with her after their respective showers, he could feel Juliet's discomfort. At first she fidgeted, tossed and turned. Obviously, being back in a bed reminded her of the attack. He wasn't sure what he could do, if anything, to help.

"I'll be okay. I just need to get used to it." She answered his thoughts before he could even voice them.

"I'm never going to let something like that happen again," Evan told her softly, reaching out to touch her back.

Juliet slid a little closer. He wrapped an arm around her, pulling her all the way over to his chest.

"Right now just try to get some sleep," he murmured.

It was as if her body needed a haven, a place where her mind felt safe, and Juliet was almost instantly asleep.

Long after he could hear her even breathing, Evan stayed awake, appreciating having Juliet in his arms. What he'd said to her was true. He would die before he let anything like the attack happen to her again. While they were undercover he didn't plan to let her out of his sight. But for now he just held her gently while she slept, and eventually fell asleep himself.

Evan awoke a few hours later to a knocking on his door. The sun was already up, but Juliet was still asleep. He glanced over at the clock: 6:30 a.m. Later than he had been sleeping, for sure, but still too early for someone to be knocking.

Evan reached for the Glock on his bedside table, easing away from Juliet's sleeping form. His phone buzzed with a message.

At your door. Hurry up, sleeping beauty.

Sawyer. Evan was tempted to ignore Juliet's brother's message, but knew he'd just start knocking louder. Evan slid out of the bed, slipped on a T-shirt with his pajama pants and went to open the door.

Sawyer and Cameron. Great. But at least they had doughnuts.

"Why the hell are you two here at this ungodly hour in the morning?"

Cameron dropped the doughnut box on the table. Sawyer, quite familiar with Evan's house, began making coffee.

"We had an idea. Wanted to run it by you first before talking to Juliet," Sawyer told him.

"Do I need coffee before hearing this grand plan?" Evan wondered if he should mention that Juliet was asleep upstairs.

"It's not a grand plan so much as a safety precaution for Juliet," Cameron said. "We were talking to one of the geeks in the tech department..."

"Excuse you, I happen to sleep with the head geek from the tech department every night," Sawyer said, pouring himself a cup of coffee from the pot before it was even finished brewing.

"Okay, so you guys were talking to Megan, and she told you what?" Evan asked. Megan was Sawyer's genius fiancée, who had recently come to work for Omega.

"Tech has developed a short-range tracker/emergency response initiator that is virtually undetectable, even with a scanner, or someone monitoring frequencies," Cameron replied, pushing Sawyer out of the way so he could get his own coffee.

"And you want Juliet to have it."

"Yes." Both men said it at the same time.

"An added safety measure for everybody. Plus, it would probably make her feel better about the entire operation," Cameron stated.

Evan nodded. Even though he had no plans to let Juliet out of his sight the entire time they were on Cady's property, a backup safety measure was never a bad idea.

"She's going to do fine. Although she's been getting a string of emails from some sick secret-admirer-type bastard. So this distress mechanism Megan designed might help Juliet more than you even thought."

"What the hell emails are you talking about?" Sawyer demanded. Both his and Cameron's posture stiffened.

"They're not actually coming to Juliet, they're addressed to Lisa Sinclair. Creepy stuff that mentions specific details about her attack last year. I'll show you." Evan got out Juliet's laptop and showed her brothers what she'd been dealing with for nearly a year.

Sawyer dropped into a chair. "Why didn't she tell us about all this?"

Evan shook his head. "She said she didn't want to put

a burden on anyone. That we had 'real' cases we were working on."

Sawyer's expletive was ugly. "That's the most asinine thing I've ever heard. This stalker thing is obviously escalating. Look at how many more there have been in the last three months. And that ratio quadrupled in the last couple of days."

"I know." Evan gave a long exhalation. "I don't like it. As soon as we get the drone codes situation under control with Cady, I'm going to make this top of my priority list."

Cameron had been leaning against the counter, silent since Evan had shown them the emails. He spoke up softly now. "She shouldn't have had to go through this alone. Not after what she's been through. I'm going over to her house right now to talk to her."

Evan put out an arm to stop him. "Cam, that won't work."

"I'm her brother. She'll let me in. I just want her to know she's not alone in this."

Evan sighed. "She's not at her house."

"Where the hell is she?" Sawyer asked. "Is she back at Omega again? She spends too much time there."

"No," Evan said, and cleared his throat. "She's upstairs. Asleep. In my bed."

Evan watched as the two men he had been friends with for over fifteen years looked at him as though he was an adversary. Sawyer stood next to Cameron, both glaring at Evan.

"What do you mean, she's up there in your bed?" They studied his clothes. Obviously, Evan had also been sleeping when they had gotten there a half hour ago. It didn't take them longer than the average three-year-old to put the details together.

"What the hell are you doing, Evan?" Sawyer's words were quiet, making them all the more menacing.

"Did she want to go to bed with you or did you push it?" Cameron's voice wasn't as quiet.

Evan's whole body tensed. "You two are my best friends in the world, but you better watch what you say right now. I would never put Juliet in a situation like you're suggesting."

Sawyer's breath flew out in a huff, and he relaxed against the counter. "Damn it, we know that, Evan. It's just, first the undercover work, then those emails, and now you tell us she's sleeping with you."

"It's too much, too soon," Cameron agreed.

"She wasn't *sleeping* sleeping with me. You both know she and I can't go under at Vince Cady's house with her cringing every time I touch her. So we've been spending as much time as possible together in the last thirty-six hours."

Evan thought mentioning her house and the shape it had been in probably wouldn't help the situation overall. Her brothers would feel the same way she had at first. As if there was no way she could handle the case.

"She can handle the case," Evan said, as much to himself as to Sawyer and Cameron. "I believe that."

"You be careful not to let things get out of hand, Evan. Don't take it too far."

Evan reminded himself that these were Juliet's brothers. Brothers who loved her very much, which was why they were being so overprotective. But they knew him, knew how long Evan had carried a torch for their sister. They just didn't like that anyone would care that much about her.

"You know how I feel." Evan snapped his mouth shut and reached for the coffee, to give himself a moment to formulate his words.

"How you feel about what?" Juliet's voice chimed in from the kitchen doorway.

Evan stopped, frozen. How much had she heard?

"Hey, little sis. We were just talking about some tracking and emergency equipment the tech department has come up with," Cameron said.

Thank God. Evan really didn't want to get into his feelings for Juliet, with two of her brothers sitting in his kitchen, while he was wearing his pajama pants. Juliet, thankfully, had changed out of the T-shirt and boxers she had slept in, and put on yoga pants and a sweatshirt before coming downstairs.

Sawyer hugged his sister. "Yeah, Megan came up with something we'd like you to wear while undercover. It's a tracking and distress device. Only good short-range, but completely undetectable. Perfect for while you're at Cady's house."

"We were dropping by to see what Evan thought of it. Didn't expect to find you here this early in the morning." Cameron's eyebrow rose.

Juliet flushed just a little bit, but she was used to dealing with her brothers. "It's not what you think."

"So Evan assures us."

Evan poured Juliet a cup of coffee and handed it to her. How he wished it *was* what it looked like. Nothing would make him happier.

Chapter Fourteen

Getting rid of her brothers took a couple hours. Juliet loved them, she really did, but they were ridiculously overprotective. When her oldest brother was around it was even worse, although Dylan was usually the most reasonable. He understood, by experience, that sometimes no matter how traumatic the event, you just wanted to be left alone.

Juliet definitely didn't want to talk with her brothers about being in bed with Evan. No matter how innocent it had been.

And definitely didn't want to talk about how good it had been to lie there with him.

She had avoided sleeping in a bed all these months because of her fears. But being in one with Evan, she'd found her fears hadn't really crossed her mind. She'd been too busy thinking about him. About how close he was and how good he smelled.

And how she was nervous about being in the bed with him, but it was a *good* nervousness, not a bad kind.

And how she wanted to kiss him again. And more.

She knew Evan had lain in bed last night, so close, and watched her. But it was because he was worried about her, not because there was any real interest on his part.

This was all just part of a critical case for him. Undercover work. She needed to remember that.

But Juliet was definitely beginning to wish it was more.

She looked over at him, dressed all in black now, as she was, ready to go do the reconnaissance work at Cady's house. There were others who could handle it, providing details about the outside of Cady's house and his security. But both Juliet and Evan felt it important to do it themselves.

She looked forward to it, actually.

They weren't really going onto the grounds, just nearby, to see what they could see. Covered by darkness, they would be counting guards, getting a lay of the land, so to speak. Juliet suspected this entire escapade was for her benefit, and she didn't mind.

"You ready?" Evan asked.

"Yep."

"Okay, we'll need to park a couple of miles away. We're not sure how far out Cady's guards patrol. We don't want to take any chances."

They drove one of Omega's cars rather than Evan's Jeep, since it would be less recognizable.

"Have you got the tracker Megan and her tech people made?"

Juliet reached down and grabbed the locket hanging around her neck. "It fit in here perfectly, even behind the picture. It's crazy how thin that thing is."

"Yeah, well, Megan's mind is pretty amazing."

Juliet didn't bring up how she had once accused Megan of working for the very enemy Megan now worked so hard to defeat. She knew how in love Sawyer and Megan were; Juliet had never been happier to be wrong.

"Let's just hope we don't have to use it tonight," she said, looking out the window as they drove into Anne Arundel County.

"Such a huge criminal sitting right under the navy's

nose. Hard to believe, isn't it?" Evan parked the car. The Naval Academy was only a few miles away.

"Cady has a lot of gall being right out here in the open," Juliet said as she got out of the car.

"He's very selective about whom he deals with. That's why we've never been able to get close to him. I'm still amazed he approached Bob Sinclair in the first place."

Juliet asked, "Are you worried? Do you think Cady is suspicious?"

"He hasn't survived this long without being so. But I don't think he's any more suspicious of us than he is of anyone else."

Juliet wasn't sure if that made her feel better or worse. "Let's hope it stays that way and that I don't do anything to freak him out."

Evan squeezed her hand. "You won't."

They left the car and walked through the shadows until they reached the top of a very small hill just outside the gated property line of Vince Cady's estate. From here they had a pretty clear, although not complete, view of the house and grounds. But there shouldn't be any danger of them being caught.

They both stood silently, using night vision goggles to study the premises for a long while. Juliet counted two sets of three roaming guards passing by every eight minutes.

"Do you see the ones on the roof?"

She moved her focus upward. "Roger that. Looks like two sets of two."

"Yeah. That's a pretty well covered place. Cady definitely isn't taking chances."

"If we have to get out of there in a hurry, it's going to be nearly impossible."

"I know." Evan's voice reflected all the solemnity Juliet

felt. It was going to be more important than ever that she keep it together and do her job.

"Let's get the amplifier planted."

Juliet followed Evan down the hill, closer to the wall that surrounded the property. They needed to get the device as near as they could without it touching the structure, which probably had some sort of sensor.

"Why does it need to be so close?" Juliet asked quietly.

"It helps amplify the signal of your tracker, but it also contains a small explosive. Not enough to do any real damage, but enough to cause a distraction if we need it."

"That makes me feel a little better." Sometimes being just a couple seconds ahead of everyone else was enough when you were undercover.

They weren't expecting a guard on this side of the wall, so far away from the others, but evidently Cady even had someone patrolling the exterior. Juliet's gaze flew to Evan's as they heard him coming toward them.

The guard was alone and talking on his radio, so evidently he wasn't aware they were there. But that wouldn't stop him from bringing this whole operation crashing down on them if he caught them.

He'd be directly on them in just a second.

Juliet felt a moment of panic as Evan grabbed her by the waist, spun her around and pushed her to the ground. Knowing he was trying to get them under the cover of a fallen tree, she slid back as far as she could, and he scooted with her. She didn't let the fear overwhelm her. It was Evan this close to her; it was okay.

He didn't have time to turn around before the guard came by, which left Juliet and Evan in a lover-like embrace. She quickly pulled her dark sleeves over her hands and wrapped her arms around Evan's neck, trying to cover as much of his exposed skin as possible.

Both of them were silent as the guard passed by only feet from where they hid. He began walking away, then stopped.

Juliet's heart hammered in her chest. Had he seen them? Could he have possibly seen the amplifier?

Evan's arm moved just the slightest bit, and she realized he was removing his weapon from his shoulder holster. There was no way Juliet could get to hers, the way they were wound together, bodies pressed up against each other from chest to toe. And Evan was facing the wrong direction to shoot.

His hand skimmed up to where her arms were wrapped around his neck. Silently, he pushed his Glock into her hand.

If the guard became a dire threat, Juliet was going to have to be the one to take him out.

There was no doubt the man was armed. Like the other patrols they had seen, he carried a modified HK-33 submachine gun. The guard might have orders to shoot on sight. Hopefully, it wouldn't come to that, but Juliet had to be ready.

Evan trusted her to be.

Why was the guard still stopped? Did he see something? Sense something was off?

Juliet relaxed minutely against Evan when the man lit a cigarette in the darkness. He didn't know about them at all; he was just trying to get away with having a smoke on the boss's dime.

Evan and Juliet waited as the guard took drag after drag on his cigarette. Although Juliet didn't relax, she knew there was no way he would be casually smoking if he suspected there was anyone hiding nearby.

Evan obviously knew it, too. Because Juliet could feel his fingers begin to trace up and down her back. All of a sudden she was very aware of all the places their bodies were touching.

All the places.

Evan ran his hand down her spine and splayed it over her hip, pulling her the slightest bit closer. His hot breath rushed across her neck.

The guard finished his cigarette and reported in on his radio that all was clear and he was headed to the south end of the property.

Juliet and Evan didn't move from where they lay, although she relaxed the arm that held the Glock. Evan's hand remained on her hip, his hard body pressed up against hers.

She couldn't hold back a little sigh when she felt the breath against her neck turn into little kisses there.

Evan rolled onto his back, but didn't release her, so she rolled over on top of him. Neither spoke as he threaded his hands into her hair and pulled her lips down to his.

There was no hesitation, no faking, no fear. Only heat. Evan kissed her as though he couldn't get enough of her. A knot of need twisted inside her.

They broke apart from the kiss, breathing heavily. This was neither the time nor the place to give in to what they were feeling. Evan pulled her in for one more brief kiss, then got up from the ground and helped her up, too.

With a minimum of words they set up the amplifier/detonator close to the wall and began the trek back to the car. They saw no sign of the guard.

Juliet handed Evan's weapon back to him. "I'm glad I didn't need to use this."

"Yeah, it would've been weird kissing you with a dead body lying right next to us."

Juliet rolled her eyes at Evan's black humor. "Not to

mention the two dozen guards that would've been chasing us once they heard my weapon fire."

They reached the car and Evan turned to her, cupping her cheek. "You did good, Jules. You kept your head, didn't panic, didn't fight me when we had to roll under that log."

"Well, I was pretty scared."

"It's all right to feel scared. It's what you *do* when you're scared that's important. You handled it like a trained agent. Nobody can ask for more."

Juliet didn't say much on the way back to DC. There was too much she was thinking about. Evan was right; she had handled the situation with the guard well. She hadn't panicked, not even when Evan had grabbed her and all but threw her down.

Because her mind was used to Evan. Not him throwing her to the ground, but him being around. His presence. His touch. Even his smell.

Evan had been gentling her over the past two days as if she were some sort of wild mare. Accustoming her to his touch, getting her mind to accept his presence as normal.

And although Juliet didn't like to compare herself to an animal, damned if it hadn't worked. After a split second of fear, she hadn't even worried about Evan's proximity; had only focused on the real danger: discovery by the guard.

The scene kept playing through her mind as they returned the borrowed car to Omega Headquarters and headed back to Evan's town house. For the first time Juliet felt assured about her abilities as an agent as they went undercover at Cady's mansion tomorrow. She might not be completely up to speed, but she would be able to get the job done. They would be able to recover the drone codes before anyone was killed.

She and Evan walked through his front door. He took off his jacket and hung it over one of the kitchen bar stools.

How had Juliet never really noticed how ripped Evan was? His black T-shirt didn't do much to hide the muscles of his biceps, pecs or abs. Thank God.

Evan turned to the fridge for a couple water bottles. He took a big sip out of one, leaning back against the counter.

"You want?" He held up a bottle, his dimple showing with this smile.

Looking at him, Juliet realized she did indeed want.

Evan. Right now. Tonight.

She knew he wanted her, too. That much had become evident while hiding under the log. This wasn't just an undercover op for Evan. *She* wasn't just an undercover op for him.

This time she didn't plan to take no for an answer. She had let the attack steal too many months of her life. She didn't plan to let it have even one more day. She wanted Evan and she knew he wanted her.

What was that saying? Leap and the net will appear.

Juliet leaped.

She slid her own jacket off and walked over to him. "Yeah, I want." She took the water bottle out of his hand and put it on the counter.

She pressed herself flush against him and reached up to wrap her arms around his neck. His hands instantly moved to her hips. She pulled his lips down to hers.

Yes. Finally. That was what she had been craving. His warm lips against hers. Evan tried to keep it soft and light, but Juliet had no interest in that. She pulled him hard against her and stood up on her tiptoes so she could get even closer.

"Juliet," Evan murmured against her mouth. "I'm not sure we should—"

She became even more aggressive in her kiss. "Not sure we should what?" Juliet finally asked.

Evan broke away just for a moment so he could look her in the eyes. "I just want to make sure this is what you really want."

"I'm pretty sure I want this more than I want to continue breathing."

With that, Evan scooped her up by the waist and spun, placing her on the kitchen counter. He grabbed her hips and slid her forward so they were as close as possible. And kissed her again, stealing her breath.

Yes, this was how Juliet wanted to feel, had thought she would never feel again. Evan's lips brushed over the underside of her jaw and down her neck. She couldn't stop the soft moan.

"I've waited a long time for this," Evan murmured against her throat.

"It's been a long time for me, too." Juliet found she could say it without bad memories coming up to swamp her.

Evan pulled back a little so they were looking eye to eye. "I've wanted you for years, Juliet. But it was never the right time."

She grabbed him by the collar and pulled him closer. "Well, it's the right time now. For both of us." Then she reached down and pulled Evan's shirt over his chest and head, letting it fall to the ground. Heat coursed through her. Everywhere their bodies touched was on fire.

Evan didn't say anything, just swung her up in his arms and carried her to his bed.

Chapter Fifteen

Evan lay in bed, watching Juliet curled up next to him, sound asleep. His mind was blown by their lovemaking a few hours before. Better, hotter, just plain more awesome than he would've ever expected.

He had tried to keep himself on a tight leash. If Juliet had any moments of panic, he wanted to be able to stop and help her through it.

But evidently the only panic she'd experienced had been about him not getting their clothes off fast enough. A couple steps up the stairs, while he was carrying her, she had been running her hands all over his chest and kissing his neck. He'd stopped right there, lowered her, backed her up against the wall and kissed her thoroughly. She'd pulled her own shirt off, and he'd made quick work of her bra, so they could be skin to skin.

Nothing had ever felt so right in his entire life.

"If we don't cut it out, we're never going to make it to the bed," he'd said.

The most beautiful smile he'd ever seen had lit up Juliet's face. "I don't want to make it to the bed. I want to make love right here, on the stairs."

Evan had been more than happy to oblige. In fact, he'd almost ripped their clothes off in an effort to oblige.

They had finally made it to the bed, afterward, with a

stop by the shower first. Now Juliet was sleeping and he needed to do the same. Tomorrow they'd be heading to Vince Cady's mansion.

Juliet's phone chirped on the nightstand by her side of the bed. That chirp—the one that signified Lisa Sinclair had received another sweetheart email. Evan tried to reach over and grab the phone before it woke Juliet, but he felt the tension flood through her. She'd already heard it.

"Just leave it," he told her as she reached for the phone.

"I can't." She was wide-awake. "Not knowing what it says makes me just as crazy as knowing."

Evan doubted that, but knew he couldn't stop her.

Sweetheart, we'll be together soon. Don't worry about your husband, I have special plans for him. He doesn't deserve you.

Evan hated the way fear crept back into Juliet's green eyes. She didn't openly panic, but the stress and tension had obviously returned.

"Jules, it's going to be fine."

"But now it looks like he's targeting *you*, Evan. And the last thing we need while we're undercover with Cady is some freak trying to track us down for some alone time with me."

"Well, we know the two are unrelated, so for now let's put the emails on the back burner. Once we finish with Cady, then we can concentrate on tracking down whoever is sending them."

Juliet looked uncomfortable, but nodded. "Okay. I'll turn off my phone notifications for that email account. I'll still get them, and so will the tech peeps at Omega, but we'll only see them when I choose to open them."

She set the phone down and Evan pulled her against

him. "That will be better. You'll be able to concentrate on the case, rather than worrying about the emails."

"You're right," Juliet whispered. "It's just, they freak me out. Throw my mind to crazy places. Sometimes it's hard to come back from that."

Evan kissed her on the forehead. "I know, baby. But you don't have to battle this alone anymore. I'm going to be here to help you every step of the way. Not to mention all three of your dumbass brothers."

Juliet smiled at that, as he had hoped, then pushed him back against the pillows and swung her leg so she straddled his hips.

"You know, we have to be at Cady's house in just a few short hours. We better get some sleep," she told him, but her wicked grin said something much different.

"Later," he growled, pulling her mouth down to his. "There'll be time for sleep later."

JULIET'S SOBS WOKE EVAN. For a moment of sleep-induced confusion, he forgot where he was and thought he was having another nightmare, with Juliet's agony in his head. But he quickly realized the sobs were coming from Juliet herself, asleep in his bed, dressed only in one of his T-shirts.

Her fitful thrashing and quiet sobs broke Evan's heart. He had hoped her nightmare days were behind her, but he also knew recovery was never a straightforward line. Steps backward were also part of the process. All he could do was keep his word and show Juliet she wasn't alone any longer.

Because she damn sure would never sleep on a closet floor again.

"Juliet." Evan kept his voice even and didn't touch her, not wanting to cause her further duress. "It's Evan, baby. Can you wake up? You're safe. It's okay."

He spoke the calming words over and over, and began gently and very loosely stroking her arm. Nothing that would seem like a grasp.

At first Juliet became more fitful, but then began to relax, almost as if his words were sinking in. He hoped that was true. He would've given his own life to have saved her from the brutality that now haunted her dreams with such poignancy.

"Evan?" Juliet's eyes fluttered open.

Thank God. "Yes, baby. I'm right here. It's okay. You were having a nightmare."

"I'm sorry. I didn't mean to wake you. Us sleeping together was probably a bad idea."

Evan wasn't sure if she meant the actual act of sleeping or their lovemaking earlier. Either way, she was wrong.

"No, it was the best idea either of us have ever had."

Juliet shrugged. "I'm not a great sleeper."

"You have nightmares. So do I. The important thing is you don't have to wake up alone anymore. You don't have to fight these demons by yourself."

She nodded, but Evan could tell she was still upset by what had happened. He wasn't quite certain what upset her more, the nightmare or him being there to witness it. She got up and headed to the shower. Evan let her go. She needed space.

And if she stuck around his bed, he was afraid he might start talking to her about *always* being there when she awoke, and holding her through any nightmares. It was too soon to be discussing that, and it might scare her off even more.

Evan could be patient. He'd been patient for years, even before the attack. He could be again.

And besides, now was not the time to worry about the future. They both needed to be concentrating on today, and Cady and retrieval of the codes. Everything else would have to wait.

A few hours later they were on their way to the estate near Annapolis. They had stopped by Omega so Megan could fine-tune the tracker and mayday device Juliet wore.

"Okay, remember the acoustic homing signal echoes off the magnetic ray with the tracker, and vertical trajectory also comes into play if the device is utilized as part of a denotation stratagem, so that needs to be taken into consideration. But because of the alloy elements, it's virtually imperceptible to discovery," Megan, one of the leading computer scientists in the country, had told them. "Any questions?"

Juliet and Evan had just looked at each other, neither really having any idea what the younger woman had just said. Fortunately, Sawyer was there to interpret, putting his arm around Megan, obvious love in his eyes.

"What giant brain here is trying to say is that Vince Cady and his men are not going to find the device on you, but it is definitely short-range," he'd explained.

"Sawyer, that's exactly what I said to them!" Megan blinked at them through her glasses, obviously believing it.

"I know, honey," he'd responded in a stage whisper. "They're just slow. Don't worry."

The little bit of humor had been just what they needed. Juliet had turned to Evan, shaking her head, her eyes twinkling. She was ready.

They were ready.

As they pulled up to a guardhouse at Cady's property an hour later in Evan's Jeep, Juliet slipped her hand into his. He gave it a reassuring squeeze.

"Bob and Lisa Sinclair, here by Mr. Cady's invitation," Evan told the guard.

The man looked it up on a small computerized tablet, then nodded and gave them instructions on where to go.

There were a number of cars already parked near the house, all high-end automobiles. Neither the number nor the caliber of the vehicles was surprising. Cady did not deal with lowlifes. His dealings were not something small-time criminals could afford.

Especially when it came to the drone override codes. Anybody interested in buying them would definitely be a big-time player. Someone Omega would need to start keeping tabs on, if they weren't already.

Like Evan, Juliet was taking stock of the different vehicles. Some of these people would be associates they'd worked with before. Others would be new. All could be potentially deadly.

Evan pulled the Bob Sinclair cloak around him—a friendly guy, good with people, not quite the sharpest tool in the shed, but smart enough. He enjoyed creature comforts and good food, but also had an adventurous side, thus the Jeep as his chosen vehicle.

Evan could tell that Juliet was fully into her role as Lisa Sinclair. Lisa was smart—not a stretch for Juliet—but also liked to pamper herself, and cared more about her appearance than Juliet ever did. She wore expensive jewelry: a diamond bracelet, two almost gaudy rings on her hands, and of course, the locket around her neck.

Lisa's clothes were a far cry from what Juliet normally wore; her tailored pants and blouse, coupled with high heels, were quite different from Juliet's more casual jeans and sweaters. But Evan was sure Lisa Sinclair's outfit helped Juliet dig more into character.

She appeared confident, professional and no-nonsense. Evan loved Juliet's causal style, but had to admit she could pull off Lisa's look as if she was born to it. It was a turn-on, for sure.

Evan parked the Jeep, then hopped out to come around and open the passenger door. He helped Juliet down from her seat and kept his hand at the small of her back as they walked toward the main door of the house.

"You look great," he whispered.

One eyebrow arched. "Of course I do," she responded, smiling. She was already Lisa Sinclair. "These shoes are Manolo Blahnik. Any girl would look fabulous."

Evan pulled her close and kissed the top of her head, partly because he knew they were being watched and the action would be in character.

But partly because he just couldn't help himself.

A member of Cady's staff opened the door as the two of them approached the steps.

"Welcome, Mr. and Ms. Sinclair," the woman said. "Mr. Cady is expecting you. We will have you join the other guests in just a moment, but first please follow our security team."

Juliet and Evan were led to a smallish room off the foyer. One man used a wand to scan Evan, while another did the same to Juliet. Evan could see her tension at the man's proximity. She glanced at Evan and he gave her a reassuring nod. She flinched when the guard touched her shoulder and asked her to turn around.

Evan had a moment of slight panic when the wand beeped as it passed over Juliet's locket. Megan had said it was undetectable as a short-range device. Had she been wrong? Was the very thing that was supposed to assure Juliet's safety going to get them both killed?

"Would you mind removing that locket, please, ma'am?" the guard asked politely, but his tone brooked no refusal.

Juliet took a step back and removed the jewelry. Evan

hoped it was as undetectable as Megan and Sawyer claimed it was.

Juliet cringed and couldn't seem to find anything to say, so Evan stepped in for her. "That was her mother's, so be careful with it." Juliet grasped his hand, nodding.

The guard opened the locket, and after much studying, and even removing the picture that was in it, put everything back and returned it to Juliet.

"Sorry," he said. "Any piece of jewelry this size must be inspected."

"Fine, just give it to me," Juliet told him in an acerbic tone. The guard handed it to her and she returned it to her neck. "Are we free to go or are we going to be subjected to more humiliation?"

"You're free to go. Sorry for the trouble."

"I would think so."

It was easy to see why Lisa Sinclair had a reputation as being a bitch. Because she was one. Juliet, once she'd found her tongue, seemed to remember Lisa well.

The woman who had met them at the front door led Evan and Juliet into a large room with multiple windows. People were milling around, talking. Waitstaff were walking around with trays of food and drink.

With his hand resting on her waist, Evan felt Juliet's tension growing, but none of it showed in her expression. A smooth, alert-but-somewhat-bored look remained planted on her face. It was damn near perfect.

"There you are!" Vince Cady came at them from across the room. "I wondered if you were going to make it at all, after our last...encounter."

Evan shook the older man's hand. "Lisa convinced me this wasn't something we'd want to miss out on."

"Well, the lovely Mrs. Sinclair has good taste." Cady gestured to Juliet's outfit. "As always." When he bent forward to kiss her cheek, she stiffened slightly, but didn't withdraw. Cady didn't seem to notice her discomfort.

"Thank you for having us in your home, Mr. Cady," she said, her tone a nice mixture of friendly and cold. "We much prefer this to an empty warehouse or other dirty building with weapons pointed at us."

Cady's laughter was booming. "Yes, this is much more comfortable for everyone. And it's only going to get better, you'll see."

More comfortable than an entire staff providing for their every whim? Evan found that hard to believe.

"But let me introduce you to my family. This is my wife, Maria, and our son, Christopher."

Maria Cady had hard, small eyes. Her smile seemed forced, although she politely murmured, "Pleased to meet you," as she shook Evan's hand.

Definitely not the friendly type, or at all personable or charming like her husband.

Evan turned to Vince's son, only to find the younger man staring at Juliet with unadulterated lust. Juliet didn't see it, because she was shaking hands with Maria. Evan wrapped his arm tightly around Juliet's waist and pulled her up against him.

Christopher Cady turned to Evan, his face smoothing out into a blank mask, friendly even. Had Evan imagined what he'd just seen in the younger man's face?

With a smile, Christopher offered his hand to shake. "Pleasure," he said.

"Same," Evan lied. He'd definitely be keeping an eye on Christopher.

"Maria, Christopher and I must go say hello to some other guests," Vince told them. "We have over twenty coming in all. The drone codes have brought out interest from quite a few buyers."

Cady was so excited Evan was surprised he didn't rub his hands together in glee. The man obviously loved being in a position of power.

"I'm not surprised," Juliet told him. "Your reputation for having quality items and not wasting buyers' time is well known, Mr. Cady."

"Please, both of you call me Vince. We should be informal, don't you think?"

"Absolutely." Evan and Juliet spoke at the same time, then looked at each other and grinned.

"Such a lovely couple." Maria smiled at them, but the smile didn't reach her eyes.

"Please enjoy yourselves," Vince said. "Eat. Drink. We'll provide further instructions once everyone has arrived."

Vince took his scary family and began wandering toward other guests.

"So far, so good," Juliet whispered to Evan. "What do we do now?"

"Like the man said, let's eat and drink. Mingle."

"Get as much information as possible."

"Exactly." Evan winked down at her. They began working their way toward a table that held different hors d'oeuvres: the scallops wrapped in bacon looked particularly delicious. "Who should be our first targets?"

Juliet placed some food on a plate as she looked around casually. Then Evan saw all the color drain from her face. The plate in her hand fell from lifeless fingers and crashed onto the hardwood floor, shattering.

Evan rushed immediately to her side. "What's wrong?"

"That man over by the door." Juliet couldn't seem to tear her eyes away. "He's Heath Morel, close friend of the Avilo brothers, who attacked me. He could be the one sending me the emails."

Chapter Sixteen

Nausea roiled in Juliet's stomach. What was Heath Morel doing here? Although he hadn't been there the night the Avilo brothers had attacked her, everyone knew he and the Avilos not only worked together, but were close friends.

Suddenly, the sweetheart emails made sense to Juliet. Before he died, Marco Avilo could've provided details about the attack to Morel, or Robert could have, before he'd gone to prison.

Evan led her to one side of the room as concerned staff members began cleaning up the mess she had made when she'd dropped her plate. All talking had stopped at Juliet's social faux pas, but now was slowly resuming its previous volume. Eyes that had been glued to her and Evan were now starting to look away, having found nothing of interest to hold their stares.

Except for those of Cady and his son. Juliet glanced their way again and found them still gazing at her. At first she thought it was because of their duty as hosts—was Juliet okay? Had something happened to her to make her disrupt the party? But then she saw Cady look over at Heath Morel, a small smile on his face.

Juliet turned her back to them, so she was facing Evan. Had Cady planned this? Had he invited Morel, to get some sort of rise out of her?

"Hey," Evan said and bent down so they were eye to eye. "Are you okay?"

She nodded tightly, unable to say anything right at this second.

"We knew there would be people from our past here," he continued. "You're still okay. We can do this."

Juliet took a couple long breaths. Evan was right; Heath Morel was here, but nothing had changed. She could still do this. The emails didn't have anything to do with the drone override codes.

"You're right," she whispered. "I'm okay. I can do this."

Evan drew her in for a hug. "Good girl. No more throwing plates, okay?"

"Got it." Juliet turned so she was standing beside him and facing everyone in the room again. "I think Cady might have invited Heath Morel on purpose, just to see my reaction. He was looking at Morel with a weird smile a minute ago."

"Wouldn't surprise me at all. That's the kind of sick stuff Cady is known for. Even more reason not to let it get to you."

"And if Morel is the one sending me the emails? It has to be him."

Evan pulled her closer and kissed the side of her forehead. "Then we're one step closer to catching him, aren't we?"

Evan was exactly right. That was how Juliet needed to look at it. She didn't need to hide from Morel; she could use this time to draw him out.

"Thank you." The words were inadequate to describe how grateful Juliet felt toward Evan. He was helping her remember how to stand and fight, rather than run and hide. She couldn't have done it by herself.

"For what?"

"For being here. For knowing what to say. For just being you."

Evan winked at her. "No problem."

The two of them began making their way around the room, talking to different people. Most of it was just chit-chat. No one wanted to give up very much information. After all, they were competitors vying for the same prize. But Juliet made mental notes of every person there, absorbing as much detail as possible to report later. She knew Evan was doing the same.

They avoided Morel, and Juliet noticed he seemed to be avoiding them also. He didn't have anything to do with her attack—he'd been in a different part of the country at the time—but that didn't mean he hadn't known about the plan. And it made complete sense that he was the one sending her the emails.

Juliet wasn't sure if she wanted to confront the bastard or just stay away from him altogether. But putting a face to the emails somehow made her feel better. Confronting the demon she did know rather than fighting the ones she made up in her head.

And speaking of demons, Juliet always felt as if someone was watching her. It didn't seem to be Morel. He was studiously trying *not* to look at her, as far as she could tell. Juliet never could pinpoint who it might be, but she seemed to always feel eyes on her. Maybe her imagination was running away with her. It wouldn't be the first time.

And maybe it was that she was in a room full of criminals and everyone was eyeing everybody else, while trying not to make it obvious.

Vince Cady certainly seemed to enjoy playing lord of the manor, talking to everyone, holding court. Everyone was doing what they could to get in his favor, in case that would help when the bidding began.

Juliet knew the auction probably wouldn't be until tonight, possibly tomorrow morning. Until then they had to play nice. Evan certainly seemed to have no problem with that. Bob Sinclair was charming with everyone. Of course, that wasn't a stretch for Evan; almost everyone liked him. But his Bob Sinclair persona hid his fierce intelligence. People tended to underestimate him, and he used it to his advantage.

Lisa Sinclair was more silent and snooty. Juliet didn't mind not talking. It gave her a chance to study people. And not have them touch her. Although she was doing better in general, she still did not like people casually touching her. She slid a little closer to Evan.

After an appropriate time to mingle, Cady held up his hand to get everyone's attention from where he stood in the doorway. "Thank you all for coming. I know we have important business to attend to. And we will soon, I promise.

"I would like to give you a tour of my house, and show you where you will be staying," he continued. He looked at his son, who was grinning slightly and nodding. "But Christopher had a much better idea, and perfect for security reasons."

Cady waited until he had everyone's undivided attention. "I will have my staff get all of your belongings. We will be going to my yacht for the next few days and conducting all business there."

Silence reigned for a few moments before murmuring broke out. Juliet looked up at Evan, concerned. He slipped an arm around her waist and drew her closer, putting his lips against her hair as if kissing her.

"It's a test. Don't show any emotion."

The words were so soft, Juliet almost couldn't hear them. She schooled her expression into a blank mask. Lisa

Sinclair would not care if they were going on a yacht. She would just want to get to business.

Christopher joined his father and held up a small metal box. He didn't explain what it was, but Juliet knew.

The transmitter/detonator she and Evan had planted yesterday. She felt Evan's arm tighten around her waist.

"Here on land there can be security compromises, but on the yacht we can assure everyone's comfort, safety and privacy."

Both Christopher and Vince were looking around the room carefully. They couldn't know for sure it was someone here who had planted the device, and even if they did, it wasn't an item that particularly screamed police.

Lawmen didn't tend to plant detonation devices. Of course, Omega Sector wasn't your everyday law enforcement.

"Anyone not interested in joining us on the yacht may leave now. Your association with the Cady family will be finished for good," Vince proclaimed.

That certainly upped the stakes for everyone. Silence fell over the room once more.

"Well, we're in! Just point us to the boat and we're ready. It'll be like a second honeymoon, won't it, honey?" Evan broke the silence with his enthusiastic response, moving toward the doorway where Cady stood, bringing Juliet along with him.

She just plastered a smile on her face, although it was the last thing she felt like doing.

Moving to a yacht changed everything. All their plans, the information they'd gleaned from their surveillance work about Cady's security forces, all wasted. The transmitting device her brothers had given her would be worthless out in the Chesapeake Bay with no amplifier.

They'd be going in blind, with no way to contact Omega for support. They'd be totally on their own.

And Evan, instead of trying to figure a way of gracefully bowing out, had just enthusiastically agreed to be the first ones on the ship.

Things had just gone from iffy to downright impossible.

EVAN DIDN'T LIKE the yacht idea, but there wasn't any way around it, so he decided to at least make it look as if he embraced the concept.

Cady was smart. This abrupt change put everyone on edge and changed all the game plans. Including Juliet and Evan's. On the yacht Cady would have all the advantages.

They'd found the transmitter where Evan and Juliet had left it, but hadn't identified it as law enforcement equipment. It could just as easily belong to someone who had more nefarious purposes in mind.

Juliet hadn't reacted to the transmitter's appearance, thank goodness. Vince and Christopher had both been watching everyone, looking for a reaction. Evan knew Juliet couldn't be happy about this change of plans. The safety net, feeble as it was, had just been yanked right out from under them.

But there was no time to talk about it, no time to get a new game plan together. They just had to go with it and watch each other's backs.

"When do we head out?" Evan asked Cady. Hopefully, keeping up the bravado would remove all suspicion from them.

"If you will just provide your luggage to my staff, we have cars ready to take you all to the ship."

Evan nodded and led the way out of the room, arm wrapped around Juliet's waist. Others followed, while a few stayed behind to press for further details from Cady, or maybe even to bow out altogether. Good. Anyone leaving now would be one less problem for him and Juliet to deal with, while also strengthening their cover.

Evan walked with her out to the Jeep. Her pinched expression tugged at his heart, but he couldn't stop to reassure her. Too many ears around.

He got their luggage out of the trunk. Immediately, one of Cady's staff members appeared to assist. Evan freely handed them over, but knew the contents would be thoroughly searched before he and Juliet saw them again.

It was all part of Cady's plan, and it was a good one. He would now control what went onto the vessel, including weapons. This would eliminate anybody planning to double-cross him. Also, once they were out in the Chesapeake Bay, cell phone reception might be sketchy, and most certainly monitored by Cady's people.

Calling in the cavalry wasn't going to be an option.

They needed to get a message about the change in situation to Omega now, but Evan couldn't figure out how to do it without being obvious. Any call they made would be heard; texts would be monitored.

"I'm going to text Aunt Mildred and let her know that we may need her to watch the dogs a couple extra days. I don't want to take a chance on being out at sea and not being able to get a message to her. You know how she would worry," Juliet said to him, already getting out her phone.

Evan could've kissed her. As usual, Juliet was one step ahead of everybody with the plan-making. Thank goodness for the Branson family and all their crazy codes with each other.

"She'll like that we're going on a boat. You know she just went on a cruise last fall." Juliet spoke as she typed. "I need to mention to her how to turn the satellite television on, too. Just in case she wants to watch while she's there, you know, since the transmitter isn't working anymore."

It looked as if Juliet would be able to get the important info out to her brothers. They would be on a ship, Omega needed to use the satellite to locate them, and the transmitter was no longer an option.

This was a perfect example of what made Juliet such a great agent. She thought out of the box and acted quickly.

She slipped her phone back into her purse. "Okay, sent. I hope it makes it through."

"Everything will be okay, either way." Evan took her hand and she slid closer to him.

Three black limousines pulled up to take the guests to the yacht. Evan helped Juliet into the closest one.

There was no going back now.

Chapter Seventeen

The yacht was everything Evan would expect of a criminal of Vince Cady's caliber. Large, able to easily sleep the twenty guests he had invited, plus the staff and security Cady had on board.

The limos had taken them to a private boatyard near Annapolis Harbor. Everyone had been shown on board and soon they were on their way into the Chesapeake Bay, with champagne served as they sailed away.

As if they were going on some sort of pleasure cruise rather than an auction of items that could potentially cost the lives of thousands of people.

Evan had to admit he was impressed by the ship's luxury. He and Juliet had been shown to their plush stateroom. A bed filled the space, surrounded by tasteful mahogany woodwork and trim. Under any other circumstance, he would be delighted to be here with Juliet.

But the fact that the room was most definitely bugged, that all their belongings had been searched and they were in the middle of a dangerous situation with little or no backup tended to kill the romance.

Evan still hadn't been able to talk to Juliet about this new change in situation. He was sure that was part of Cady's plan: keeping everyone on edge and giving them very little privacy.

"Hey, baby, we're on a cruise. Just like we always wanted to be." Evan walked over, hooked an arm around Juliet's waist and began kissing her neck, working his way up to her ear. Her shivers delighted him, but this embrace was business.

"Room is bugged. Audio, maybe visual," he whispered.

She tensed, but then nodded and kissed him. "Well, this wasn't exactly what I had in mind. I was thinking more along the lines of the Bahamas," she said out loud.

"If we secure this deal with Cady, I promise to take you there. The commission on the drone override codes will be outrageous."

"Yeah, yeah, yeah. I've heard all that before, Bob."

"Aw, don't say that, baby." He pulled her in for another hug. "Let's take a shower together so we can get ready for tonight."

Juliet nodded. "I definitely feel like I need one, especially with some of the people Cady invited. Go turn the water on."

The bathroom was just as opulent as the bedroom. Evan switched on the shower, knowing it would be their only chance to talk privately.

Not that he minded getting in a shower with Juliet for any reason.

He undressed and entered the stall, a large walk-in one with granite tiles and a clear glass door. Evan turned the water to hot to make the glass steam. He wasn't sure if the surveillance was just audio or had a visual component, and he wanted to protect their privacy as much as he could.

Evan tried to stay focused on the case, but found it difficult when Juliet opened the shower door a few minutes later.

"Wow, this is nice. We should get something like this at home," she said, loudly enough to be overheard.

"I know. Get in here."

Evan wrapped his arms around her and brought her flush up against his body. He couldn't control his reaction to her, but forced himself to concentrate on the business at hand. This might be the only time they could talk freely with one another.

"Surveillance in the room, without a doubt. Cady wouldn't bring us all out here otherwise," Evan whispered in her ear, at a level that couldn't possibly be overheard with the water falling all around them.

Juliet nodded, but he felt her stiffen. She didn't like the thought of someone watching her naked. Neither did he. "Sorry."

"Our plan is still the same, right?" she asked. "We make sure we have the highest bid when the codes become available."

"Yes."

"What about Heath Morel?"

Morel complicated things, especially since Juliet was right—it seemed most likely that he was behind the emails to her.

"We can't let him distract us."

The water rushed down over both of them for long moments. "This is all hard enough for me. I'm not sure I can do it with him around. Just seeing him, knowing he has those sick details…"

Evan skimmed his fingers up and down her spine. "I know, but you'll have to, baby. You have to just push it aside."

He could feel her sigh against him. He didn't blame her. The whole Cady case was difficult enough without Morel thrown into the mix.

"We'll get him, Jules. I promise. Within twenty-four hours of being back on shore, we'll make sure Morel gets picked up for questioning. We'll put an end to all those emails. But it will have to wait until after. Can you do that?"

Juliet nodded her head against his chest. They stood in silence for another moment, water pouring around them. Then Evan felt her hands slide up his arms to his shoulders and link behind his neck. "I don't want to talk about Heath Morel anymore."

Her body brushed up against him. Evan's body responded in kind.

"Do you think there's any chance of cameras being inside this shower?" Juliet asked, planting kisses along his chest.

"No, not with all the steam. They wouldn't be able to see anything."

"Good," she murmured, and pulled his lips down to hers.

AFTER THEIR SHOWER, Juliet and Evan got dressed and walked around the yacht. They strolled as if they were just enjoying being out on the Chesapeake Bay, but they really wanted to glean as much intel as possible.

As far as Juliet could tell, the ship had five levels. The bottom one seemed to be staff quarters, the galley and the engine and maintenance areas. She and Evan hadn't been able to get down there at all. They'd been met by an armed guard at every entrance they'd strolled by.

The other floors held guest rooms, a large dining area, multiple decks to sit out on and enjoy the views, even a swimming pool. There was also a lounge with couches and seats. Juliet concluded that's where the auction would probably be held.

All and all, their walk gave them lots to see and admire, but very little info in terms of strategy.

Now they were back in their room, dressing for dinner. Juliet tried not to let the thought of cameras spying on them from somewhere in the room bother her, but it did. She changed clothes as quickly as she could.

Her dress wasn't formal or particularly fancy, but Juliet knew she looked good in it. The quintessential little black dress, but in a rich plum color instead, the perfect foil for her blond hair. The dress fell to just above her knees and had a slightly naughty V neckline. Nude-colored, high-heeled sandals completed the outfit.

"Wow." Evan was slowly looking her up and down. "I'm not sure we're going to make it out of this room."

Juliet smiled. "Too much?"

He shook his head slowly. "No. Definitely no. Just enough."

Juliet loved the hungry look in Evan's eyes. She never thought she'd let someone close enough to see that look again.

Evan himself looked dashing in his jeans and black T-shirt, coupled with a stylish beige sports coat. He offered his arm. "Shall we go to dinner?"

Juliet hooked her arm through his. It was almost as if they were on a date, except for the being on board a ship miles from land, with over a dozen known criminals.

The plan while they were at dinner was for Evan to corner Morel and make some barely veiled threats about the emails. After all, Bob was Lisa's husband. He wouldn't like for her to be receiving emails of that type from anyone.

She'd already received three more since her arrival at Cady's house this morning. The emails were escalating in number, in tone, in desperation. Juliet had turned off notifications for when she received an email, but she was still able to check them manually, which she'd done just before dinner.

She and Evan had gone over them together. And while they no longer caused that sick feeling of dread to course through her, she still hated reading them. Especially hated the word *sweetheart*.

Hopefully, Bob's talk with Morel would eliminate the email problem altogether, or at least while they were working this case.

Dinner went smoothly, with Vince Cady announcing that the auction for the different items, including the drone codes, would take place the next afternoon. After dinner, they were herded, gently and tastefully, of course, by the staff into the large sitting room. It opened out to the water and people milled around with their drinks and desserts.

Juliet spoke with Maria Cady for a while, mostly just polite chitchat. The woman seemed very tight-lipped. Juliet wondered how much she knew about her husband's business. Did she know what was really going on here? Did she deliberately turn a blind eye? Ultimately, it wouldn't really matter.

Juliet noticed Evan talking to Morel across the room. Part of her wanted to go over and stand by Evan while he let Morel have it, but the bigger part of her wanted to stay away from the man completely. Just looking at him brought up memories of the Avilo brothers, making her stomach turn.

Juliet gave a polite excuse to Maria and went to stand outside near the railing. It was peaceful out here, darker and cooler, with no need to talk or even listen to other voices. Juliet breathed in the fresh night air and her stomach settled. She could handle this.

The sound of a match being lit just a few feet away startled her. She turned and saw Christopher Cady's face as he brought the flame up to his slim cigar. He took a couple steps toward her.

Juliet started to back up, but forced herself to stop.

Don't panic. You're fine.

"Enjoying the peace and quiet out here?" Christopher asked.

He's just a man talking to a woman. Making conversation. Don't *panic.*

But tension suffused her body. "Yeah, it's a nice night and it got a little stuffy inside. So I decided to come out so I could be alone." Juliet hoped he would get the hint.

But no. Instead, Christopher took a step closer. "It's beautiful out here, isn't it? I love boats. They can take you to lots of private places, romantic places."

Juliet just stared at the man. Lisa Sinclair was *married*, for heaven's sake. Was Christopher hitting on her? She took another step farther away. Unfortunately, this led her into a little more darkness.

Even more unfortunately, Christopher took another step toward her. Juliet looked over to the main room where everyone was talking and mulling around. No one, not even Evan, was looking this way or paying her and Christopher the slightest bit of attention.

"I think I'm going to go back inside," Juliet said. She didn't want to be rude to Vince Cady's son, but didn't want to stay out here alone with him, either. He gave her the creeps, and the sweet smell of his thin cigar soured her stomach. "Bob will wonder where I am if I stay away too long."

Christopher leaned forward and grabbed her arm where it rested on the railing. "Bob is a fool to allow you to be out here alone at all. No one should leave a woman as beautiful as you unattended."

Juliet's panic spiked at the feel of Christopher's hand on her. But she forced herself to ease away rather than yank. "I have to go."

"I would like you to stay and talk to me. I can tell you more about the boat. There's lots of interesting facts about it you don't know. Of course, some are better shown."

Juliet turned away. "No, thanks."

But Christopher wasn't interested in taking no for an answer. He grabbed her arm again, just above the elbow. Juliet cringed, her flesh crawling. She forced herself to take a cleansing breath in through her nose and out through her mouth. "I'm really not interested. Please just leave me alone."

Christopher's darkly handsome face took on a cruel look. "I'm Vince Cady's son. If you want any sort of chance at winning the auction tomorrow it would be in your best interest to be nice to me."

What he said was probably true, but Juliet didn't care. She couldn't stay there with him even a minute longer without retching all over the place. She twisted out of his hold. "I have to go."

This time Christopher grabbed her shoulder in a painful grip. Juliet's reflexes took over. She turned slightly into the stronger man's grasp, then rammed her elbow into his solar plexus. She heard the breath whoosh out of him, but didn't stop. Instead, she grabbed his arm with both hands, pulled him closer and, with a yank and shift of her body weight, flipped him over her back.

Before Juliet even realized what she was doing, Christopher Cady lay gasping on the yacht's wooden deck, staring up at the sky.

Chapter Eighteen

It happened faster than she thought possible. Juliet still held Christopher's wrist, now in a grip that would allow her to break bones if he tried anything else. Reflexes still in full-alert mode, she looked around for any potential threats.

But all she saw was Evan rushing toward them. And a dozen concerned faces behind him. And the Cady security team.

"Hey, what's going on here? Lisa, is everything all right?" Evan asked her.

She immediately let go of Christopher's hand. Awareness of the situation crept into her brain. Oh no, what had she done? Probably just cost them the case, maybe worse.

Evan stepped around Christopher and stood right in front of Juliet, offering them a little bit of privacy from the prying eyes with his body. "You okay, honey?"

He trailed a finger down her cheek, but didn't try to embrace her. Juliet appreciated the distance. "He grabbed me and instincts just took over. I'm so sorry." She stared down at her feet.

Evan tipped her chin up with one finger. "It'll be fine. He shouldn't have grabbed you." Evan took his sports coat off and wrapped it around her shoulders. Juliet didn't even realize she had been trembling. She snuggled into the warmth.

Evan turned around to face Christopher, who was now sitting up on the floor. Security guards were rushing to assist him.

"I'm taking my wife back to our cabin. As I'm sure you now realize, she doesn't like people to grab her. I trust nothing like this will happen again."

Christopher didn't say anything, just glared at them. Evan returned to where Juliet had propped herself against the railing, put his arm around her and led her away.

The magnitude of what she'd done hit Juliet. She brought her fist up to her mouth. "Oh no, Evan, I've ruined everything." She couldn't help it; tears welled in her eyes. "What's going to happen?"

He stopped and pulled her into his arms. They were far enough away now that no one could see or hear them. "Hey, we'll deal with it."

"But I assaulted Cady's son! I may have just blown everything."

"He wasn't hurt, you just knocked the wind out of him. It's late. Let's head back to the room and let everything die down."

Juliet nodded. She couldn't think of any way to undo the damage she'd done.

"My brothers were afraid something like this would happen. They were right."

"They were right about what? That you would be able to handle yourself if some guy started forcing his attention on you? Christopher Cady won't make that mistake again."

"I guess not," Juliet whispered, but she didn't feel any better. What if, after everything they'd done to get here, she and Evan got booted off the ship because she hadn't been able to keep her cool?

"You just need to get some rest, Lisa. Everything will

feel better in the morning," Evan said a little too loudly as he opened the door to their cabin.

Juliet took the hint. It wasn't safe for them to talk anymore, at least not about blowing the case. But even Lisa Sinclair would be worried about the ramifications of assaulting Cady's only son.

"I'm worried what Vince is going to do when he finds out."

Evan nodded and gave her a little squeeze. "We'll deal with that as it comes."

EVAN COULD TELL Juliet didn't get much sleep. Her tossing around had little to do with the patch of rougher waters the boat had hit and everything to do with her apprehension over what had happened with Christopher Cady.

Evan should never have left her alone. His talk with Heath Morel, trying to get the other man to agree not to send any more emails to Lisa, had been pretty fruitless, anyway. Morel had played his cards very close to his chest, refusing to admit to any knowledge whatsoever about the emails. And Evan hadn't wanted to make a big scene that would get them noticed, so force was out of the question.

Which was about the time he had looked up and seen Christopher Cady flying through the air over Juliet's shoulder. Evan's immediate concern had been for her safety. Had Cady assaulted her? Tried to harm her in some way?

But once Evan made it over there and realized Juliet wasn't harmed—and neither was Cady—he'd also been concerned for the case. Although he'd tried to assure her otherwise, Juliet was right to be worried about how Vince would respond to her aggression against his son.

But it was already morning, so evidently Cady wasn't planning to kill them. He would've done that last night, although even for Cady that was a bit extreme. But Evan wouldn't be surprised if they were put off the ship altogether, or at the very least not allowed to participate in the auctions.

Which would put the drone codes out in the open. They couldn't allow that to happen.

But hell if Evan had any sort of plan B.

A sharp knock at their cabin door startled Evan and had Juliet sitting up in the bed, clutching the sheet to her chest. Evan looked around for anything he could use as a weapon, but there wasn't much. He pulled his jeans on and answered the door.

"Yes?" He opened the door the smallest crack possible.

It was one of Cady's security force. "Mr. Cady would like to extend an invitation for you to join him for breakfast in his private dining area in one hour. I'll return then to escort you."

The man didn't wait for an answer; just turned to leave. Evan closed the door and found Juliet up and already starting to get dressed.

"Breakfast with Cady. Is that bad or good?"

Evan honestly didn't know. "We'll just have to see and go from there."

True to his word, the guard was back to escort them an hour later. Evan and Juliet hadn't said much to each other during that time. There wasn't much that could be discussed when they knew their conversation would be overheard.

Her expression was tight and she kept biting at her lip as they walked toward Cady's dining room. Evan wished he could reassure her, but had no idea how.

"Good morning, Bob, Lisa," Vince said to them as they were shown into the room. He sat at a small table that held settings for four. "Please sit down."

Coffee and juice were already on the table, but no food

had arrived. Evan held out a seat for Juliet, then took the one next to her.

Juliet glanced quickly at him, then turned her attention to Vince. "Mr. Cady, please allow me to apologize for what happened with your son last night. I am afraid I still have some…residual issues from some…occurrences in my past."

Vince didn't respond, just added some cream to his coffee.

"Mr. Cady," Juliet continued, "I hope you will take into consideration that it was only me who assaulted your son. Bob had nothing to do with it. He wasn't even with me at the time."

Evan stared at her. What the heck was she doing?

"I don't blame you if you want me to leave. But I hope you will not penalize Bob, or the people we work for, because of my actions. Please allow Bob to remain for the auction today."

Cady turned his head and looked at her while stirring his coffee. "You assaulted my son."

Damn it. Evan knew he should've stepped in before now. *Assaulted* was such an ugly word. "Mr. Cady, my wife—"

"I'm just trying to tell you that it was me. It had nothing to do with Bob." Juliet cut him off.

Cady leaned back in his chair and took a sip of his coffee. "No offense, Mrs. Sinclair, but you don't look like you would be big or strong enough to assault anyone. Much less someone as large as Christopher."

Juliet started to speak again, but Cady held out his hand to silence her. "Furthermore, I know Christopher well, and I have no doubt that if you flipped him over your shoulder, then he did something to deserve it."

For the first time since last evening Evan could relax slightly. Cady wasn't mad. He was impressed with Juliet.

"I just don't like to be touched, once I've told somebody not to."

Cady took another sip of his coffee, laughing. "That's right. No means no. Well, you've certainly helped Christopher learn that lesson. One I'd hoped he'd learned, but evidently had not."

Two waiters brought out trays of food, setting plates before each of them. "My wife was going to join us, but she's not feeling well because of the rough waters." Cady was referring to the empty chair. "Please go ahead and eat."

Evan was a few bites into his delicious meal of eggs, bacon and fruit when Christopher Cady walked in. When he saw Evan and Juliet his expression turned from bored to irritated to smug.

"You wanted to see me, Father?"

Evan saw Juliet's fork hesitate halfway up to her mouth. Did Cady expect her to apologize to Christopher? She would do it to save the case, but Evan wasn't sure he could stomach it. He reached over and grasped her free hand.

"Mr. Cady—"

Cady held out a palm to silence Evan.

"Christopher, I was just speaking to Bob and Lisa about what happened last night."

The younger Cady could barely tear his gaze away from Juliet to answer. "A misunderstanding, Father. I'm sure Lisa did not mean any harm by what happened."

"I'm sure you're right. You, on the other hand, I cannot speak so confidently about."

Now Vince had Christopher's attention. A growing awareness of his father's feelings about the situation dawned over his dark features. And he wasn't happy about it.

"Father—"

"Christopher, I want you to apologize to Mrs. Sinclair for your behavior last night." Vince cut him off without even waiting to hear the rest of the excuse.

At first Evan thought Christopher would refuse, defying his father. But then he turned stiffly to Juliet. "Please accept my apology. It was never my intention to hurt or frighten you in any way."

Juliet nodded, but didn't say anything. There wasn't anything she really could say. Christopher returned her nod and turned to leave, but Vince stopped him.

"I want you to apologize to Mr. Sinclair, too. After all, it was his wife you traumatized."

Evan caught Juliet's concerned gaze. She knew, as he did, that this was going too far. Evan didn't understand all the dynamics between father and son, but obviously there was some sort of power struggle going on.

Evan had not expected—or wanted—an apology from Christopher. Neither had Juliet. The best both of them had hoped for was just not having to abandon the case because of what had happened. Evan wasn't sure what buttons Vince wanted to push with Christopher, but wished it didn't involve him and Juliet.

"Mr. Cady. That's not necessary. Truly." Evan tried to defuse the situation.

"Oh, I think it is," Cady replied, while casually eating his breakfast. Obviously, putting his son in this humiliating situation didn't bother him at all. The opposite, in fact.

Christopher stared at his father for a long moment, then finally turned to Evan. "Then my apologies to you also, Mr. Sinclair."

The words were calm, but his gaze murderous. Evan wasn't sure if Christopher directed the sentiment toward him or toward his father, but knew he'd just made an enemy.

But this wasn't Evan's first enemy. It wouldn't be his last.

Vince evidently decided his son's lessons in humility were over, because he didn't stop him as he turned again to leave.

"There, glad we got that settled," the drug lord said as he took another bite of his eggs Benedict.

"Well, thank you for understanding, Mr. Cady," Juliet said to him. Evan noticed she wasn't really eating, just pushing her food around on the plate. He didn't blame her. He'd lost the taste for his.

"Vince, please, Lisa. Call me Vince."

"Vince." Juliet smiled at the older man, but the smile didn't reach her eyes. Her instincts were right. Vince Cady wasn't to be trusted.

Cady lifted his water glass. "Here's to a fruitful business partnership for years to come."

Juliet and Evan both lifted their glasses. Evan gave his own silent toast: *Here's to the day we take you and your entire enterprise down, you bastard.*

The clinking of glasses was sweet to his ears.

Chapter Nineteen

The auction late that afternoon wasn't very different from other ones for art or antiques. It certainly wasn't like the cattle auctions Evan had been to a few times as a child, with a guy up front speaking very rapidly and with a Southern accent. This was much more subdued.

Some people were here bidding on items for themselves that they would either keep or sell later. Others were representatives of a specific buyer. They were authorized to bid up to a certain amount and no more. Bidding was tricky; definitely an art form.

Acquiring the drone override codes would be difficult. Although not everyone would be bidding on them, there were at least three parties who were here specifically to do so, Evan knew. Omega had given him and Juliet an unlimited ceiling for bidding for the codes. After all, Omega would recoup the money when Cady was arrested and his accounts frozen in the next few months, after Evan had a chance to glean as much information as possible about the drug lord's associates and suppliers.

Keeping the codes from reaching the streets was critical, but just as important was figuring out how and from whom Cady had gotten them in the first place. That's why Omega hadn't just taken the drone codes by force. They needed Cady's connection inside the military. Undercover work was the only way to figure out who that was. If Evan and Juliet didn't win the codes in the auction, then Omega would have to move much more drastically. Figuring out Cady's supplier would no longer be an option. It was better if Evan and Juliet could just buy the codes. Their cover would remain intact to use as long as possible.

Never burn a cover if you didn't have to.

But bidding was a skill. Going in with an extremely high bid would do nothing but throw suspicion on Evan and Juliet. They would need to use all their cunning in the bidding process. Win, but make sure it looked close.

Evan was ready to get this all over with. There were just too many unknowns on the yacht. Things he couldn't control. The situation with Vince that morning was just plain weird. Christopher had seemed ready to kill them at any moment. And Heath Morel being here had Juliet in a frenzy.

Potential for disaster abounded. And although Juliet thus far had held up pretty well, better than most people would have under the circumstances, Evan wanted to get her off this ship and back in a situation where they had more control. Maybe not the upper hand, but at least *a* hand. Right now it felt as if he was trying to do everything with both hands tied behind his back.

Not to mention the storm had really picked up and was rocking the yacht, even with its powerful stabilizers, all over the place. Almost everyone had a slightly green tinge.

Evan looked around for various items as the auction continued, some art of questionable origins, and weapons, both legal and illegal. These weren't what Evan and Juliet were here for, although every once in a while they would bid on something just to shake things up a bit.

Another piece of artwork came up for auction. Juliet sipped at the champagne a waiter, struggling to keep glasses upright on his tray, had provided. "I'm going to bid on that," she murmured.

Evan turned to study it more closely. "Why? Do you know something about it I don't?" She had learned a lot in the past year as an analyst, Evan knew. She had deep knowledge of many more cases than just the ones Evan worked on. Perhaps this piece of art held some importance.

"I know it's hideous."

He looked over to find her smiling at him. "And that's why you want to buy it?"

"Yeah, you could hang it in your bathroom."

Evan grasped her hand and linked their fingers together. He gazed at the painting more closely. It really was ugly.

"Um, yeah. Maybe we should pass on that. Save us the paperwork and explanations later."

"Oh, all right. I'm disappointed."

Evan smiled to see Juliet relaxed enough to make a joke. Keeping a firm grip on reality was important when undercover. Despite the mishap with Christopher last night, she seemed to have rebounded quite well.

"You're doing great." Evan leaned over and kissed her temple, whispering the words in her ear. "Hang on just a few more hours and we'll be done here. You're amazing."

Juliet smiled at him crookedly. He knew she didn't believe him. He wished he could make her realize how amazing she really was.

The bid for the drone codes came up, drawing Evan's attention away from Juliet. This was it.

The bidding started slowly. Everyone's attention focused on this big-ticket item regardless of whether they were bidding or not. Evan could see Vince Cady watching the proceedings closely.

A pair of Ukrainian buyers were their biggest competition, according to the rumors Evan had heard over the past day. They were buying for themselves, leaving clear ideas of their intent. To do as much damage as possible to their enemies, which included the United States.

Right now the Ukrainians were being bid up by a young man with a Caribbean accent Evan had met briefly. He knew this was just a Hail Mary for the younger man. He had no real shot at winning.

Juliet was in charge of bidding for them. She sat, looking almost bored, as the action continued, not putting in a bid at all.

"Planning to jump in at some point?" Doing nothing made Evan nervous.

"I have a plan. Just simmer down." Juliet winked at him.

Evan sat back in his chair. He didn't exactly relax, but one thing he had learned was that when Juliet had a plan, it was almost always a good one. He kept telling her to trust herself. Now was his chance to show her that he trusted her, too.

Juliet did nothing as the Ukrainians continued to bid, forcing Caribbean Accent out of the running. Evan thought surely she would jump in then, but it was Heath Morel who bid instead.

Juliet tensed, but didn't say or do anything. She and everybody else watched as the bidding went back and forth like a Ping-Pong match between the Ukrainians and Morel. Evan wanted to prod her to get in there, but forced himself not to.

Juliet could handle this.

The bidding slowed down and began growing in increments of five thousand dollars rather than the twenty thousand just moments before. Juliet made her play. She raised her hand to get the auctioneer's attention and made a bid one hundred thousand dollars above the current price.

A collective gasp echoed through the sitting area. Cady

grinned, all but rubbing his hands together. Morel turned to glare at Juliet, and Evan slipped an arm around her shoulders for support.

The bidding was now too high for Morel. He stormed out of the room. The Ukrainians bid again, five thousand higher than Juliet's huge bump. She countered with fifty thousand dollars more.

No gasps this time, just silence. Juliet had obviously proved herself as the person to be beat in this auction. Evan turned to watch the Ukrainians argue with each other in short, quiet barks. One obviously wanted to keep bidding. The other recognized the truth: Juliet was going to win.

She'd handled it perfectly. Throwing around the exact amount of money to stop the bidding cold. Letting the others know she was serious, but not seeming wasteful. As she'd told him, she'd had a plan. And it had worked.

The Ukrainians finally shook their heads at the auctioneer. He asked for any other offers, waited a few moments, then closed the bidding. Juliet now owned the drone override codes.

Evan's relief was palpable. Their biggest obstacle had just been overcome. Cady walked up to congratulate them, Christopher by his side.

"Well bid, my dear," Vince said, holding out his hand to Juliet. She gave it to him, but instead of shaking it, he brought it to his lips.

Evan could see Juliet didn't like the feel of Cady's lips on her skin, but she held it together.

"Thank you, Vince. Sometimes it just takes a woman's touch."

"And a very deft one it was. Although it seems like you've made some other people quite unhappy."

Evan noticed that Christopher had inched closer to Juliet. Evan wasn't sure whether it had been done on purpose or not, but he still didn't want the younger man anywhere near her. Evan slipped an arm around her and pulled her against him, farther from Christopher.

"Some people are sore losers," he told Vince.

"I'd like to know some more about the people you buy for," Vince said, while leading them toward the dining area. Now that the bidding was complete, dinner would be served. Although it looked as if neither Morel nor the Ukrainians had much of an appetite. They were nowhere to be found.

"We buy for different people at different times," Evan told Vince.

"But none of our clients like us to talk about them." Juliet smiled charmingly at the Cadys.

"And that is why you are so good at what you do." Vince returned Juliet's smile, but his was much more calculating. This had probably been a test to see if the Sinclairs kept their heads, and their mouths shut, even when feeling a little cocky, having just come off a win.

"It's a shame you've been out of the game for so many months," Christopher said.

Juliet wrapped her arm more tightly around Evan as the boat rocked again, and looked up at him. "Bob and I just needed some time to ourselves."

"And why was that?" Christopher asked.

Evan didn't know why the man was pushing this point, but was determined not to give him anything to use against them. "Everybody needs a break sometimes. Plus, can you blame me for wanting to spend more time with someone this beautiful?" He bent down and kissed Juliet's cheek.

Vince chuckled. Christopher seemed less amused. "Yes, if I had someone so lovely I would never let her out of my sight," he responded stiffly. "Excuse me."

Christopher walked toward some of the other guests.

"Ignore my son. Maria spoiled him as a child and he has not had such good luck with the ladies," Vince told them. "He lived in Europe until recent months, near his mother's family. He's had a difficult time adjusting to American culture."

Evan winked at Vince. "Not everyone can be as charming and witty as you and I, Vince. Know what I mean?"

Juliet rolled her eyes. Vince chuckled ruefully. "Well, he is my son. Someday all of this gets handed down to him, so I'm trying to teach him as much as possible." He looked toward where Christopher had stormed off. "But often it's difficult."

Evan slapped Vince on the back. As both Bob Sinclair and Evan Karcz, he was thrilled that they'd won the auction, and wasn't afraid to show it. "Ah, kids today. What are you going to do? Let's get a drink."

They enjoyed dinner, sitting again at Vince's table. Evan told stories of growing up in Virginia and the trouble he'd gotten into as a kid. Almost all the stories were true, just with names changed or certain facts left out. That was always the best bet when working undercover. Keep your stories as close to the truth as possible. The fewer lies to remember the better.

His lightness caused Vince to open up a little, which was what Evan had hoped. Although the older man didn't say anything they would directly use against him when the eventual arrest and prosecution occurred, they were one step closer to entering Cady's inner circle. It wouldn't happen today, maybe not anytime soon, but eventually Evan would be the one to bring this bastard down.

And a friendly dinner with lots of laughs didn't make Evan forget that. Vince Cady was a criminal. Had killed, at the very least indirectly, through his sales. But probably directly, as well.

"Shall we head back to my cabin? I can present you with the drone override codes, which I'm sure you'll want to authenticate. Then you can transfer the money."

Chapter Twenty

Evan met Juliet's eyes as she glanced at him sharply. This would be the opportunity for them to get a message to Omega—coordinates letting headquarters know exactly where they were, in case emergency extraction became necessary, although it didn't look as if it would. He and Juliet had done pretty damn well on their own. But they hadn't checked in for over twenty-four hours. Evan knew Juliet's brothers were worried.

"Sure, Vince, let's do it." Juliet smiled and put her napkin down next to her plate.

Evan stood and helped her with her chair. She took his arm and they followed Vince out of the dining area, stumbling slightly at the rough seas.

Angry eyes drilled into their backs as they left the room. Could be the Ukrainians, could be Heath Morel, could be Christopher. The list of people angry with them grew by the hour.

Vince's cabin was much larger and more elaborate than theirs. The sleeping space was tucked away from sight and a sitting area with beautiful views and a private deck took up over half the room. Two guards stood just outside the door. No one got in or out without them noticing.

Cady motioned for them to sit in the chairs, left for just

a moment, then returned with a briefcase in hand. "Here you are, as promised. The drone override codes."

Cady undid the clasps, revealing a computer attached to the outer casing. It was obviously military grade or something damn close. He typed in a few passwords and the specs of a drone appeared on the screen, as well as a number underneath.

"I assume whoever you're buying for already has access to the Department of Defense mainframe. Without that, these codes won't be of much use. I can, of course, provide that for your client, but it would be a separate charge and would take a little more time."

Juliet took the briefcase from Cady, smiling ruefully. "It's not our first time playing in the big leagues, Vince. We'll take care of the DOD mainframe for our client." She made a tsking noise.

The drug lord chuckled, obviously charmed by her. "Just checking, Lisa. I never miss out on an opportunity to make money."

"I don't blame you. Sometime you'll have to tell me how a businessman like you can get access to the DOD mainframe."

"It's always who you know, my dear. Always who you know."

A knock on the door interrupted them. Christopher walked in.

"Ah, son, I'm glad you're here. We're just about to finish the transaction. Mrs. Sinclair is validating the codes."

Christopher nodded and remained standing just inside the door.

"Is it okay for me to call our client? I'm assuming you've lifted the signal that's been blocking cell phones since we left port?"

"An important security measure," Vince told them. "But, yes, you are free to make your call now."

Juliet brought out her cell phone and dialed a number. She knew every word she said would be overheard both by Vince right now and probably someone else on his security force monitoring all cell phone traffic coming into or leaving the yacht.

"Do you mind putting your call on speaker, Mrs. Sinclair?"

Juliet didn't even hesitate. "Sure." She pressed a button and set the phone on the table in front of her.

Although Cady was all smiles, and even the sullen Christopher looked neutral, Evan knew this was yet another test. One wrong word from Juliet or anyone on the other end and everything they'd worked for would be blown to bits.

As soon as someone answered, Juliet began speaking. "This is Lisa Sinclair calling on an unsecure line for Mr. X."

There was a moment of silence. "Yes, please hold."

Christopher Cady's lips pressed into a white slash. Obviously, he had hoped to get a least a name out of the conversation. Juliet noticed his annoyed look. "Sorry, we have security measures of our own."

Vince still appeared relaxed as they waited for "Mr. X" to pick up. Evan prayed it was someone from Omega intimately detailed with the case. He imagined the scramble going on at Omega headquarters as they attempted to determine the best person to talk to Juliet.

As the silence dragged out, Christopher spoke. "It sounds like Mr. X doesn't have time for you."

"Mr. X is an important man. If it is taking him a while to get to the phone, I'm sure he has his reasons."

Such as tracking this call, Evan knew. Omega would have started running the trace as soon as the call came in.

"Perhaps we need to just give the drone codes to the next highest bidder, Father. Since the Sinclairs can't seem to get in touch with their buyers."

Juliet tried her charm on the younger Cady also. "Christopher, I assure you, Mr. X will be on the line momentarily. We've been out of touch for a couple of days, so he wasn't expecting my call just now. Give it a few more moments."

Christopher didn't look convinced, but didn't say anything further.

Finally a voice came on the line. "Lisa. You've been out of touch for some time now. I was beginning to get a little frantic."

It was Juliet's brother Cameron.

"My apologies, Mr. X. There was a change in plans, although I must admit I ended up on a lovely yacht. As a matter of fact, I'm sitting right here with the yacht's owner."

Evan knew Cameron would take the hint.

"I see. And with Bob, too, I hope. Or have you thrown him overboard?"

"No, I'm still here, Mr. X. Enjoying my time with my lovely wife," Evan responded.

"And were you able to secure the items we discussed, in the midst of what seems like a mini-vacation?"

"Yes, sir," Juliet said. "Even came in under budget. I have the first of the codes to be authenticated. Once that is done—and I'm sure there won't be any problem—the money can be transferred. Is Dr. Fuller nearby, sir?"

Why did she want Sawyer's fiancée to be there?

"I'm sure she's around here."

"You'll need her to access the code. She's the one able to do what needs to be done, in terms of authentication. She'll know what to do with the code. I'll be sending it to you, and the account number to route the money, right after our conversation."

"Well, good job, as always, Lisa. And you, too, Bob. When can I expect to see you again?"

"Soon, sir. We've enjoyed the boat. Water is turning a bit choppy, but nothing too rough."

"Do I need to send a lifeboat to rescue you?" Cameron asked.

Evan and Juliet both laughed lightly, but they knew what Cameron was really asking. Were they in trouble? They weren't. But getting these codes into safekeeping would definitely be a good idea.

"Well, if you happen to have a lifeboat nearby, that would be great. Otherwise I guess Lisa and I will just suffer through the gourmet food and fine company a couple more days," Evan interjected.

Cameron pretended to laugh, too. "I'll see what I can do. But it looks like you're being well taken care of."

"We're just glad to have the codes for you, sir. Getting them to you is the most important thing." Juliet was on the same page as Evan. If they could get those codes off the ship tonight, that would be the best thing for everyone.

"I'll have Dr. Fuller authenticate, then we'll transfer the money. Tell your seller to expect it within the hour."

"Thanks, sir. Transferring the data now. See you soon."

Juliet disconnected the call. "I'll just email this code and your account number in an encrypted file. Like Mr. X said, it shouldn't take long."

She sat down with her phone and began sending the information.

"Lisa's pretty amazing, isn't she?" Evan told the other men. Vince smiled, but Christopher just glared at him.

Vince was right, his son definitely did not have much going for him when it came to the ladies. That was okay;

soon he'd be rotting away in prison with his father. His lack of game wouldn't matter then.

"Okay, finished." Juliet turned to Evan and nodded. He wasn't sure exactly what she'd just sent to Cameron, and wished he could get her out of this room so they could discuss it. But he didn't want to leave without the rest of the codes.

"Great." He held out a hand to her as she stood. The ship was beginning to take on more movement now from the waves outside. Juliet was looking a little green from the rocking. Evan knew his own coloring probably wasn't much better. They walked over to the balcony so they could get some air. Ominous clouds hung low in the sky. The sun was going down, although finding it was nearly impossible given the cloud cover. It wasn't raining yet, but would be soon.

"You doing okay?" Evan asked her. Vince and Christopher could hear them, so there was no opportunity to talk about important stuff yet.

"I'll be better after we get the confirmation we need."

It didn't take long, thank goodness. The Cadys were already antsy enough, especially Christopher. Juliet received the text.

"Okay, your money is in your account. You can check it," she announced.

Christopher sat at the laptop at the table. A few moments later he confirmed it. "It's there, Father. Everything looks good." He stood back up.

Evan took Juliet's arm. "Okay then." He grabbed the briefcase with the codes. "We're going back to the upper floors, where maybe this rocking isn't so bad. It's been a pleasure doing business, Vince."

He turned with Juliet to leave, and for a moment thought

Christopher was going to stop them, but the younger man just looked at her before stepping aside.

Juliet clung to Evan's arm as they walked down the hallway.

"I sent our coordinates to Cameron. Megan should be able to decipher them amid the numbers, especially if she knows she's looking for something," Juliet told him.

That's why she had asked if Dr. Fuller was around. Juliet had wanted to make sure someone would recognize the coordinates. Sawyer's fiancée would be sure to spot them.

"Good. Hopefully, they'll come tonight, so we can at least offload the codes. We should get those into safe hands as soon as possible." They couldn't take a chance on them being intercepted during an electronic submission. The codes needed to be handed off person to person.

Evan grabbed a railing to help with balance. This storm was turning nasty. Rain and nightfall made getting around even more difficult.

"Let's just head back to the room. There's no point staying out here," he muttered.

Juliet nodded. "Okay. We have until 3:00 a.m. before whoever Omega is sending will be here. They'll be at the back of the ship."

"How do you know that?"

She held up her cell phone. "Message from Cameron or Megan or whoever from Omega ended up sending it. It says 'Code received and verified. Money deposited in given account. Further contact can be made through Mr. Stern, extension 0300.'"

Evan smiled. "Stern of the boat, zero three hundred hours. Very clever."

"I know." Juliet grinned at him. "I'd forgotten how much I like this part. The thinking on my feet, figuring out ways around barriers."

Evan brushed a strand of her now very wet hair behind her ear. "You've definitely got a natural talent. I hope you'll think about that for cases in the future."

She shrugged. "Maybe. I know I'm doing better. I'll think about it, that's all I can promise."

"Sounds reasonable to me. Now let's get back to our cabin. I think a hot shower would be in order to warm us up after all this rain."

"Absolutely." Juliet grabbed his arm. "And we definitely should take one together. I'd hate to be wasteful."

Evan loved the heat building in Juliet's eyes, but also the smile he saw in them. He picked up speed, leading them to their cabin. "Yes, let's go do our part in saving the planet."

Chapter Twenty-One

Juliet awoke to find someone's hand over her mouth. Terror flooded her. Her eyes instantly flew open, but she couldn't make out much in the dark room. One thing she knew for sure, Evan wasn't in the bed next to her.

She immediately began fighting, grasping her assailant's wrist and attempting to pull him closer so she could hit him. But she couldn't get a good angle to strike, so began to claw at his face. Juliet heard a foul curse as her fingernails found skin.

It was so similar to her attack by the Avilo brothers. Juliet still couldn't see who was in the room. Was it Heath Morel?

No matter who it was, she wasn't going to allow it to happen again.

Juliet struggled against the hand that held her head pinned to the mattress. She attempted to pull her legs around to gain a better position.

And where was Evan? He'd been in bed with her when they'd gone to sleep a few hours ago. He wouldn't have left without telling her.

Juliet scratched at the face again. The hand was removed for just a moment, but before she could make any sound, a fist crashed into her cheek. Blood filled her mouth.

Juliet fought to hold on to consciousness while the world

spun and weaved. From across the room she heard a muffled ruckus, but couldn't see what was going on. Was it Evan?

A crash and then silence. Had Evan been hurt? Juliet renewed her efforts against her attacker. She rolled quickly off the side of the bed, landing on her feet. She was able to get off two sharp kicks to the attacker's midriff, but then the boat lurched and she lost her balance. Her opponent took advantage and Juliet received another blow to the jaw.

This time she couldn't hang on to consciousness. She moaned as blackness closed in around her.

When she awoke she was being tied to a chair. They weren't in the cabin any longer; it looked as if they were in the ship's galley. Evan was tied to another chair, unconscious, still in his sweatpants and shirt, his head bleeding from a nasty gash near his temple.

And it wasn't Heath Morel who had done this. It was the Ukrainians. One was tying Juliet, the other keeping watch at the galley door.

"Vince Cady isn't going to stand for this, you know. His men will be here any second to break up this little party." Juliet tried to make the words as clear as possible, but it was difficult with her swelling jaw.

"I don't think Mr. Cady is going to know about this at all. At least not until it is too late." The man's accent was thick.

"Our room was bugged. Cady's men are probably on their way right now."

"You mean bugged with these?" He held out two transmitting devices in his hand. "I'm sure Mr. Cady's security team will figure out there is a problem, but will most likely blame it on the storm."

Juliet was afraid they were right.

"We want the drone codes," the man said.

"Look, maybe we can talk about a sale. But Bob and I spent our buyer's money to get the codes. We can't just give them to you. Our reputation would be shot." Juliet knew she needed to stall. To come up with a plan.

"More than just your reputation will be shot if you do not provide us with the codes. Or maybe not shot." The man pulled out a knife, but instead of using it on Juliet, he walked over to Evan's unconscious form. "Let's see if we can get your husband to wake up."

He began poking his knife into Evan's shoulder. Not deep, but enough to cause the wounds to bleed through his shirt. Evan moaned and began to awaken.

"Look, fine, stop, okay?" Juliet struggled against the zip ties that held her to the chair, but there was no give. She saw Evan's eyes open, glazed over in pain. The Ukrainian poked the knife into his shoulder again, twisting it. Evan's lips clamped together and he sucked air through his nose.

"Stop! Okay? Just stop," Juliet pleaded. She couldn't stand to see Evan in that much pain, but she knew she couldn't give the codes to the Ukrainians. "You need the briefcase Cady gave us."

Juliet didn't tell him that they'd already downloaded all the drone codes off the computer that was inside the briefcase and wiped the computer clean. She and Evan had put the codes on a hard drive in preparation to handing it off to Omega at 3:00 a.m. It now rested inside Juliet's pillowcase.

What time was it now? Maybe she wouldn't have to rely on Cady's security team to get their act together. Maybe the Omega agents would soon be on board. When Juliet and Evan didn't meet them at the rear of the ship, the agents would come looking for them, right? That's what Juliet's brothers would do. Although she knew Omega wouldn't be sending Sawyer or Cameron. The wounds they'd sustained recently would prevent them from scaling the side of the yacht.

Juliet glanced at the clock on the galley stove. Only a couple minutes after two. Damn it, it was too early for the Omega team. The Ukrainians would have Evan chopped up into pieces by three.

"This briefcase?" the man asked. He had it on one of the kitchen counters.

Damn. They already had it here. This was going to play out quickly, not giving them the time Juliet had hoped for. She looked over at Evan. More blood oozed from his shirt at the shoulder.

Think.

Juliet watched as one of the Ukrainians opened the briefcase and booted the small computer. She knew it wouldn't take him long to figure out there was nothing on it.

Think!

She racked her brain. Yelling wouldn't help. They were in the galley, distant from the rest of the ship. Plus the storm was too loud for anyone to hear much. She was going to have to find a way of getting them out of this on her own. The first thing she needed them to do was untie her from this chair. Until then, she was useless.

The man turned from the computer to glare at her, his lips pulled back, teeth bared. "It does not boot up. There is no information on here."

"Damn it." Juliet did her best indignant impression. "Cady must have double-crossed me."

The Ukrainian stared at her in silence for a moment, then in one fluid motion took the two steps to her and backhanded her across the face.

Juliet's head jerked all the way to the side and blood flew from her mouth, spraying onto the floor. She could feel her eye already beginning to swell shut from the ring the man wore.

"I will waste no more time with you!" In his anger, the accent became thicker.

The man grabbed his knife from the table and walked over to Evan. He took the wicked blade and jammed it into the front of Evan's already injured shoulder, this time much deeper.

Evan couldn't control the groan that escaped him. Juliet watched as all color drained from his face and sweat began dripping down his brow.

The Ukrainian turned back to her. "Again?" he asked. "Your husband is much tougher than I gave him credit for. I think he can take it."

"Lisa, no…" Evan could hardly get the words out.

The Ukrainian pulled his knife out, causing Evan to give an agonizing gasp, and raised his arm again.

"No!" Juliet screamed.

"Then you will tell me where the codes are."

"Yes," Juliet sobbed the word. "They're in our cabin."

"Tell me where."

She knew if she told him, she and Evan would both be dead. Not to mention a known enemy of the United States would possess drone codes that could cost the lives of thousands of innocent people.

"I have to show you. It's a hidden safe and has biometric coding. Only Bob or I can open it." The lies flew out of Juliet's mouth, but at least it would get her out of this damn chair.

"Fine." The Ukrainian came and cut her loose. He turned to his partner and spoke in their native tongue. The other man nodded, grinning evilly.

"I just told my partner that if we are not back with the codes in fifteen minutes, he is to kill your husband. By gutting him from top to bottom with his knife. Slowly."

Both men laughed. Juliet's stomach turned. She nodded.

The Ukrainian kept her close by his side as they left, knife poking into her ribs. He made sure she could feel the blade.

Juliet had no idea what she was going to do. The chances of her being able to take down this hulking beast in fewer than fifteen minutes, and then defeat his partner, were remote. Both were armed and probably waiting for her to try something like that.

They walked down the empty hallway in silence. Her captor led her to a service elevator at the rear of the ship. None of the guests would be out at this time of night, especially not in the middle of a storm.

The elevator was empty, as expected, but Juliet could see some water pooling on the floor in one of the back corners. A wet person had been in this elevator recently. As inconspicuously as she could manage, she touched the wet wall and then brought her fingertips to her lips.

Salty.

Juliet had grown up in Virginia and vacationed at the Chesapeake Bay her whole life. And her mother, a high school science teacher, had always used every opportunity to teach her children—even during vacations.

The Bay was a unique water source, an estuary. It started with fresh water north of Baltimore, but by the time it got south of Annapolis—where they were now—the water was brackish, becoming more and more salty.

In this storm, anybody could've made a watery mess in the elevator. But only someone who had just come out of the Bay would've made a *salt*water mess.

Omega agents were on this ship.

For the first time since she'd come on board, Juliet had a sense of hope. She needed to be ready, and prayed that

Omega had sent a good agent. She wished Sawyer and Cameron weren't injured and that Dylan wasn't retired. Her brothers were the best the agency had to offer. But of course, right now Juliet would take even a rookie straight out of Quantico.

The Ukrainian didn't notice anything suspicious. As the elevator doors opened, he grabbed Juliet's arm again and pressed the knife against her ribs. They walked this way down to Juliet's room. She didn't have a key and just reached for the doorknob.

"Glad you guys had the good sense to leave the door unlocked," she said, just a hair too loudly. Wherever the Omega agent was, she wanted to make herself as noticeable as possible, without making the Ukrainian aware of that, of course.

Her captor shoved her into the room. "Why do you waste time? Perhaps you want to be a widow and allow my partner to viciously kill your husband? Maybe I'll just sit here and let the minutes count down."

"No." Juliet shook her head. "No, please."

"Then where is this hidden safe you mentioned?"

"I lied. There is no hidden safe."

The Ukrainian stepped toward her, his nostrils flaring, his skin mottled. "Then I hope you enjoy pain, and that your husband does, as well. You will suffer mightily before you die."

"No, I have the codes. They're right here, look." Juliet walked over to her pillow and retrieved the drive from the case. She tossed it to the Ukrainian. He inspected it, then looked back at her.

"Good, now you do not need to suffer. But unfortunately, you still need to die."

Chapter Twenty-Two

The Ukrainian came barreling toward Juliet, knife extended. She grabbed the pillow off the bed—it wouldn't help much, but at least it was something—and shifted her weight sideways as the large, beefy man came at her. She used the pillow to help push the Ukrainian to the side, using his own momentum against him. He stumbled, but didn't fall all the way to the floor.

Juliet knew this would be her only chance for escape. She ran toward the door, but the Ukrainian was too quick. He grabbed her ankle and yanked, pulling her down. She tried to kick him off, but he was stronger. He reached over to grab his knife and Juliet knew this was the end.

She opened her mouth to scream, not knowing if it would be heard in this storm, but she had to try. The sound hadn't even left her mouth when the door slammed open and a figure dressed from head to toe in black neoprene flew through the air, tackling the Ukrainian. Juliet backed away, out of reach of the knife.

She couldn't see his face, but knew the Omega agent was here.

The Ukrainian was determined to kill this new arrival. The agent, on the other hand, at first used nonlethal blows, but when it became obvious they weren't going to work, the man's stance altered.

Juliet could see the change, recognize the training. The Ukrainian didn't know it yet, but he was a dead man. And this Omega agent? He definitely wasn't a rookie.

It was over in a matter of moments. The Ukrainian came at his attacker, knife aimed at his heart. The agent twisted and stepped out of the way, flipping his foot out and tripping him. Then he straightened quickly and knocked the other man forward with his elbow. The Ukrainian couldn't recover his balance.

He fell to the floor, landing with his own knife in his chest, dead just seconds later.

The agent whipped his hood off and ran to Juliet. Shock pooled through her.

"Dylan?"

What was her oldest brother doing here? He wasn't even an active agent anymore, for heaven's sake. Not that you could tell that from the fight that had just occurred.

Dylan put his face next to Juliet's and spoke almost silently. "Is this room under surveillance?"

She shook her head. "Not in here. It's been dismantled."

He pulled her into a hug. "Jules, are you all right? Where's Evan? You've got a load of bruises on your face. Are you hurt?"

"What are you doing here, Dylan?"

He gently framed her face with his hands. "Juliet, are you hurt?" he repeated.

"No, I'm fine. I'm fine. Just some bruises. But I have to get back to Evan. That guy's partner—" she pointed to the body lying on the ground "—has instructions to kill Evan if we're not back in about five minutes."

"I'll help you with the other guy."

"Dylan, why are *you* here?"

"When Cam and Sawyer told me about the yacht and all the changes yesterday, I flew in to headquarters to see if there was anything I could do. When we got your message, both Sawyer and Cam wanted to be the ones who came here, but neither were up to the physical aspect of getting on board."

"Didn't Omega have anyone else to send?"

"Of course they did, but we weren't sure what condition you would be in. Everyone thought it would be best if a family member met you, in case there was…trauma."

Juliet quickly hugged him. "I'm fine, Dylan. Trauma-free. Although I was probably about to get myself killed by that guy. Thank you, by the way. You may not be an Omega agent anymore, but nobody would've known it from what I just saw."

He bent and kissed her on the forehead. "You look great, little sis, um, except for the massive bruising and swelling."

Juliet rolled the eye that wasn't swollen shut. "Thanks."

"No, I mean you seem together. Prepared. In charge. You look better than I've seen you look in eighteen months."

"I'm doing better, Dylan. I really am. Evan was right, I just needed something to force me to get back in the game."

"Karcz being right, now there's a first." Dylan winked at her. "Let's go get him."

She opened the door, but when she heard voices down the hall, immediately closed it again. "People are out there, Dylan."

She handed him the hard drive with the codes. "Here, you take this, find your other Omega guy and move out. I'll get Cady and his security people to help me with the other Ukrainian and Evan."

"Are you sure? I hate to send you to Cady for anything."

"No, it will be fine. Vince will be furious that the Ukrainians tried this right under his nose. I'll tell him I killed this guy. It will work."

"Okay. Be safe, sis. See you soon." Dylan kissed her forehead, then pulled his neoprene mask back over his face. Juliet opened the door and headed toward the voices she heard, while her brother made his way in the other direction. Halfway down the hall, she turned to check Dylan's progress, but he was nowhere to be seen.

Omega had lost a brilliant agent the day they had lost Dylan Branson. But Juliet knew he had his reasons for quitting.

Knowing he was clear, she started screaming her head off.

"Help! I need help!" Forcing hysteria wasn't difficult.

Juliet was sure she looked a sight—bruised, bleeding, screaming, in her T-shirt and torn yoga pants. It didn't take long for everyone to find her. Security, guests, even Vince and Christopher Cady were soon in the hallway, despite the late hour.

Juliet grabbed the biggest guy in the corridor, pretty sure he had to be part of the security team, and started dragging him toward the galley.

The fifteen minutes was almost up and she was afraid the other Ukrainian might already be torturing Evan with his knife, even if he hadn't killed him.

"The Ukrainians are trying to kill us. One has my husband in the galley." Juliet tried to make the words as clear as possible, but her mouth felt like mush from the punches she'd taken. The security guy had drawn his weapon, so evidently he understood the gist of what she was saying. Another security person was attempting crowd control, trying to get everyone to return to their assigned cabins.

Juliet left them behind, running down the hall toward the elevator. The ride down the three levels seemed to go on forever. She didn't waste time talking to the guard. The moment the door slipped open just enough for her to fit, she was through. The guard was right on her heels.

Juliet barreled through the galley door, instantly taking stock of the situation. Evan was alive, but the Ukrainian stood in front of him, knife raised. Juliet didn't hesitate, didn't take even a moment to consider her own safety, just threw herself at the thug before he could figure out what was going on and harm Evan.

She took him to the ground, where they landed side by side, legs entangled. Juliet steeled herself against the pain of the collision, but found it difficult to see straight. The big man was quick to shake off the effects of the fall, and before she knew it, his knife was raised and coming toward her.

Evan yelled her name and she prepared to block the knife.

Until a shot was fired and the Ukrainian fell backward, a bullet hole in his forehead.

Juliet pulled her legs out from under the dead man's and looked over at the galley door. She expected to see the guard with a raised weapon, but instead it was Christopher Cady who had shot the Ukrainian. The gun was still in his hand, his arm still raised.

Juliet didn't care who had killed the other man. She was just glad to be alive and that Evan was, too.

She got up and stumbled over to him.

"Damn it, woman, are you all right? What the hell were you doing, tackling him like that?" Evan looked like hell. Half his shirt was bright red with blood from his shoulder.

"Are you okay?" She wasn't sure if she should apply pressure to the wounds, or if that would just cause him more pain without really helping him. "Somebody cut him loose."

One of the guards immediately sliced the plastic ties

that bound him to the chair. Evan wrapped his arms around Juliet, pulling her into his lap. "Where's the other psycho?" he whispered in her ear.

"Dead. In our room. Long story."

"And the codes?"

"Safe in the place they need to be. In good hands. Even longer story."

Evan raised his eyebrow at that, but said nothing. Juliet was sure that, like her, he was just glad something had gone right in this whole brouhaha.

Vince Cady made his way over, followed by his son. The older man looked aghast. "Lisa, Bob, I cannot believe this has happened while you were under my protection. My men are already investigating. It looks like the Ukrainians went to great lengths to circumvent our security measures."

Juliet noticed Cady didn't mention having the rooms bugged, only "security measures."

"Yeah, well, the other member of that merry little gang is dead in our cabin. Thanks to the storm, he tripped and fell on his own knife."

"Yes, he has already been found. And I am quite proud of Christopher, that he did not hesitate to do what needed to be done."

Juliet looked over at the dead Ukrainian. She was glad Christopher hadn't hesitated, either, or it might've been her lying there. "Thank you," she offered. Christopher still gave her the creeps, but in this case she owed him her thanks. She smiled and held out her hand.

He took it, but instead of shaking it, brought it to his lips. Juliet barely contained her shudder. She withdrew her hand as politely as possible.

Evan's arms tightened around her.

"Bob needs medical attention. Those psychos stabbed him in the shoulder," Juliet stated.

Vince nodded. "We have a medical professional on staff. I will have someone escort you both. You have injuries, too, Lisa." The older man grimaced as he glanced at her face. She must look pretty bad.

Vince and Christopher both left to confer with the security team, anger clear in both men's stance and tone. Vince Cady might be a criminal, but his sense of honor had been contravened, his own sanctuary violated.

Heads would roll that something like this could happen without the security team's awareness.

Juliet looked over to the doorway and found Heath Morel standing there, staring at her, malice evident in his expression. He turned and left before she could respond. Not that she'd know what to say or do.

"Are you okay?" Evan whispered, now that they were relatively alone. He obviously hadn't seen Morel, and Juliet didn't mention him. "How did you take down that Ukrainian? What the hell happened?"

"Dylan happened," Juliet murmured back.

"*Dylan*? Here on the ship? Now?"

"Well, hopefully not anymore. I gave him the drive. Omega sent him, since they didn't know what shape I'd be in. Didn't want to send a stranger."

"Then that poor Ukrainian bastard didn't have a chance."

Juliet sighed and shook her head. "My thoughts exactly."

"Are you sure you're okay, baby?" Evan stroked her bruised face, grimacing.

"Surprisingly, yes." Juliet shrugged. "Battered face notwithstanding. You were right. I can handle more than I give myself credit for."

"See? You should listen to me more often."

Juliet brushed Evan's hair away from his forehead with

gentle fingers. "You're worried about me? You're the one who got stabbed."

He kissed her gently on her bruised, swollen lips. "It's only a flesh wound. But if my arm falls off be sure to pick it up for me, okay?"

Juliet could see sweat still beading on Evan's forehead. She knew he must be in pain. But that he would worry about her and make jokes to help her feel more comfortable even now…

God, how she loved him.

Her eyes flew back to his and she drew in a startled breath. Where had the thought of love come from? After her rape, she had figured that love wouldn't be in the cards for her, that she would never again be comfortable enough with a man to be close.

But here she was, sitting on the lap of the man she trusted most in the world, as comfortable as she could ever dream of being. They were both wounded, exhausted and surrounded by criminals, but Juliet felt safe.

So maybe love wasn't such a crazy idea, after all.

"What? What is that look? You look like you've just had a breakthrough in quantum physics or something." Evan smiled, shaking his head.

"Yeah, something like that." This wasn't the place for declarations of love. But she did lean in and kiss him tenderly. "You're a pretty good husband, Mr. Sinclair."

Evan's smile got even brighter. "Well, you're a pretty good wife, Mrs. Sinclair."

They probably would've stayed there awhile, just holding on to each other, if the staff member hadn't come to lead them to the medical attention they needed.

Chapter Twenty-Three

Evan watched the distant port of Annapolis come into view. It would take only an hour or two now before they docked and were able to disembark. He was ready to get off this yacht.

He glanced at Juliet, who sat in an overstuffed love seat enjoying the late afternoon sunshine. Her eyes were closed and her battered face turned up toward the sun, which had chased away all traces of the storm. The sight of her wounded face brought back many unpleasant memories for Evan, but Juliet seemed to be doing fine.

More than fine, if her slight smile gave any hint.

Truly, she had handled the entire situation with the Ukrainians like a champ. She may have been out of the game for the past eighteen months, but no one would have known that last night. Evan could still feel the terror that had washed over him when that bastard had taken her out of the galley to go get the codes.

Not knowing what the Ukrainian was doing to Juliet—whether he would kill her as soon as he had what he wanted—had been much worse than the pain in Evan's shoulder. And then to see her come flying back through the galley like some professional wrestler, tackling a guy twice her size? Yeah, she'd saved Evan's life, but she'd also taken ten years off it as he'd watched, helpless, as the second Ukrainian raised that knife at her.

So thank God for Christopher Cady and his good aim. *That* was a sentence Evan never thought he'd say.

Vince Cady, although thrilled with his son's actions, was truly appalled at what had happened. He'd moved Evan and Juliet into a huge cabin for the little of the night that was left and had apologized profusely. Multiple times.

In the end, Evan had no doubt this incident would strengthen their relationship with the miscreant. It was always good when a criminal owed you a favor. Vince was less likely to be suspicious of them in the future when he remembered what they had gone through under his watch.

Cady would eventually be arrested for his crimes, but first he would inadvertently provide Omega all sorts of intel about his criminal network. Evan would see to that.

But most of all, everything had become crystal clear to Evan last night. He was not going to live without Juliet any longer. Life was too short, too fragile. And he'd loved her too damn long to be without her anymore. Whatever it took to convince her of that, he would do it. He'd made the mistake of giving her space for too long.

He wouldn't be making it again.

"You doing okay over there?" Juliet asked him from her chair. "How's the shoulder?"

The yacht's medic had stitched him up and given him a tetanus shot and some painkillers. It didn't seem as though any permanent damage had been done, especially since Evan had full range of motion. But the doctor had suggested he get himself completely checked out once they reached shore. None of Juliet's bruises and swelling would have any permanent effects, either, he predicted.

Evan turned and leaned against the railing so he was facing her. "Not too bad. How about you?"

"I'm just glad that ridiculous storm is over. This is much more what I think of when I envision myself on a yacht."

Yeah, they'd made it through all sorts of storms last night.

Evan went to sit next to her on the love seat. He didn't see anybody within earshot, but just in case, he pulled her close.

"How about, when we get off the boat, you come and stay with me at my town house?"

Juliet opened her one good eye. "You mean, for the op?" Her voice was barely more than a whisper. "In case they're following us?"

He shrugged, then brought his face near hers. "Yeah, that. But mostly because I want you there, Jules." He kissed her gently. "Now. When this case is over. Forever."

Juliet sighed. "I'm still pretty messed up, you know."

"We're all messed up in this business. We'll just take each day as it comes. Together." He wanted to tell her he loved her, but was afraid it was too soon, that it might scare her off. If she agreed to come stay with him, hopefully live with him, that would be enough for right now.

Evan held her close as the ship headed to Annapolis. He enjoyed just being there with Juliet. Omega safely held the drone codes. And because of their injuries, nobody was bothering them.

He felt Juliet stiffen as she leaned back in his good arm. His gaze followed hers and he realized the problem. Heath Morel. That bastard was still throwing malicious glances their way every chance he got.

Evan and Juliet hadn't checked for the past twenty-four hours to see if she had received any more sweetheart emails. But regardless, Evan had had enough of that non-sense. As soon as they were back on dry land, he was going to make sure Cameron or Sawyer picked up Morel.

The man needed to be questioned about the emails so they could get to the bottom of this. So Juliet could move on with her life. They probably couldn't actually arrest and prosecute Morel, as the emails weren't threatening in nature. But they could see him charged with other crimes.

"We'll get him, don't worry," Evan vowed. "He may not spend any time in jail for those emails, but I'll have your brothers breathing down his neck. He'll keep his distance."

"I just want to move forward. To stop having to worry about those emails and the past in general."

Evan kissed her temple. "I know, hon. And you will. We'll handle it for you. Let's just concentrate on the future."

Juliet smiled and turned her face back up toward the sun. "That's no problem at all."

A FEW HOURS later Juliet and Evan were finally off the yacht and on their way back to Omega to debrief. At the first pay phone they saw, just in case their cell phones had been bugged by Cady, Evan stopped to call Cameron and Sawyer. He wanted Heath Morel picked up as soon as possible, before the man went underground and they couldn't find him.

As Juliet had said, it was time to start concentrating on the future. The sooner they took care of Morel, the sooner that would happen.

He and Juliet both were looking forward to not having to worry about what they said or if someone was watching or listening. And he knew they both wanted to wash the filth of the past few days off them.

After they had gotten off the ship and returned to Cady's house via limousine, Cady had apologized again, Christopher right by his side, as they were leaving. "I hope this incident won't jeopardize our business dealings in the future," Vince had told them.

"It's not like you planned this," Evan had responded.

"Although next time, we trust your security team will be more on the ball." Lisa's snooty tone came through loud and clear.

"Oh, believe me, they will," Vince promised.

"And thanks again, Christopher, for your quick trigger finger." Evan shook hands with him, noting that his gaze remained riveted on Juliet.

"Yes, thank you, Christopher," she had murmured, when he'd let go of Evan's hand to shake hers.

"Au revoir," Christopher had replied.

French? Evan barely refrained from rolling his eyes. He had ushered Juliet to the Jeep immediately.

They both just wanted to go home and crash. Evan especially, since Juliet had agreed to stay at his house, but they both needed to debrief, so here they were.

They barely made it out of the parking garage and into the building before Juliet was engulfed in hugs by her brothers. All three were still there, even though Dylan didn't technically work there any longer. The eyes of each shone, locked on Juliet.

Relief and pride were evident in their every motion, every statement.

Juliet smiled at Evan from the circle of brotherly limbs and torsos. Her chin was high, her voice animated as she told some of the story of what had happened on the yacht.

Good. She deserved to be confident and satisfied in what she had accomplished. Because it was a lot, on both a professional and personal level.

After greetings, they were ushered to the Omega physician, who reevaluated their wounds. Although Evan's shoulder hurt like hell, the doc agreed with the ship's medical professional. It didn't look as if there had been any permanent damage, given Evan's range of motion. The doctor gave him a round of antibiotics and pain medication, warning him not to take the latter until he was near a bed he didn't need to get out of for at least eighteen hours.

Juliet's wounds, now a myriad of purples, greens and blues all over her face, were also superficial. Painful, but not serious.

Their boss, Dennis Burgamy, with his overworked assistant Chantelle by his side as always, found Evan and Juliet. He congratulated them on a job well done, obviously thrilled that Omega would be able to take credit for recovery of the drone codes.

Yeah, Burgamy always had his eye on the truly important stuff. Like accolades.

But at least he told them to go home and get some rest. Debriefings could take place tomorrow, since nothing involved with the case was pressing.

Evan was thrilled at the thought of sleeping with Juliet at his side. Someplace where he didn't have to watch what he said because other people were listening. Where he could actually call her *Juliet*. Although he didn't think either of them were up to anything too physical, he still just wanted to be with her. Holding her. That was more than enough to make him happy.

Of course, he didn't necessarily want to explain any of this to her brothers just yet, even if they were his best friends.

Evan grabbed Juliet's hand and pulled her around a corner, out of earshot of everyone else. "You're still coming back to my place, right?" He kissed her briefly, gently on the lips.

Juliet nodded. "I need a ride, since you drove me here.

And my brothers are going to have a field day with this, you know."

Evan rolled his eyes. "Oh, believe me, I know. I was hoping maybe not to get into all that with them tonight. I'd like to be fully functional and able to defend myself before telling them that I'm having my wicked way with their sister."

Juliet leaned in a little closer. "Your wicked way with me? I think I like the sound of that."

"Then let's get to my house." He kissed her again; he couldn't help it. It was all he could do not to back her up against this wall and kiss her until both of them couldn't see straight. Brothers be damned. Evan would take his chances.

And what was that nonsense he'd been thinking, about just holding her tonight? Not the way both of them were feeling right now.

At least Juliet still had the sense to remember that a lot of their colleagues, not to mention their boss, were just right around the corner. She pushed Evan back. "Okay, we'll just need to stop by my house and grab a few things. Then I'm all yours."

At those words, he leaned in again, but she stopped him with a hand on his chest, a playful smile on her face.

Not a moment too soon. Sawyer stuck his head around the corner. His eyes narrowed at their close proximity, but he didn't say anything about it. "Hey, Evan, Baltimore PD just nabbed Heath Morel. They're not sure what to hold him on. Cam and I were going to go question him. You want to come observe in case you can help?"

Evan sighed. All he wanted to do was go home with Juliet this very second. But the sooner they dealt with Morel and got those sweetheart emails stopped, the sooner she would be able to move on with her future.

Their future.

"Yeah, I want to come," Evan told him. "We can't let Morel see me, of course. But I can feed you info from the other side of the glass."

"Okay, we're headed out."

Evan nodded. "I'll be right there."

Sawyer left and Evan turned back to Juliet, smiling ruefully. "I guess we'll have to put those other thoughts on hold for a few hours. Here are my keys, to the Jeep and my house. I'll see you in a little while, okay?" He tucked a strand of Juliet's blond hair behind her ear, then kissed her again.

"I'll be waiting," she murmured against his lips.

Chapter Twenty-Four

A couple hours later, after Evan and her brothers had left to question Morel and Juliet had finished a little of the paperwork at Omega, she pulled up to her house in Evan's Jeep. She just sat in the vehicle looking at her home, dark and empty, for a minute. How she had hated coming here for the past eighteen months. Hated knowing she was alone and weak and a coward.

Hated knowing she'd be trying to sleep in that damn closet, like a child afraid of the monsters under the bed.

But now, after the past week, her perspective had changed. She had found her footing in the case and realized how much she truly enjoyed undercover work. She'd kept her wits about her and successfully completed a dangerous mission, possibly saving thousands of lives in the process.

Just as importantly, she'd found out she could still respond passionately to a man. At least when that man was Evan, whom she had known—somewhere in the depths of her subconscious—was in love with her. Had been in love with her for a long time.

Just as she had been with him.

They had been floating toward each other for years and things probably would've happened a lot quicker if it hadn't been for the attack. But Juliet didn't begrudge that anymore. The past was the past and she wasn't going to let it control her. She and Evan were stronger together because of what had happened. And they would remain strong.

She got out of the Jeep and made her way inside her house. For the first time in eighteen months, she didn't bolt all the multiple locks on her door when it closed behind her. She didn't have to live in fear any longer.

Juliet looked around. She liked the thought of leaving this house for good. It held too many bad memories she didn't want to battle anymore. Even if she wasn't moving in with Evan she would've been looking for a new place. Moving forward.

She didn't rush through her house. She knew Evan would be hours with Heath Morel. That was another part of her past she wanted to have done with. She was glad they'd arrested him. Her brothers would take care of this for her. For once their excessive overprotectiveness would come in handy. She didn't expect to have much future trouble from Morel.

Juliet got a suitcase out and packed clothes and toiletries. Her house was still a disaster, even with the work she and Evan had done a few days ago. But she'd deal with that later.

She grabbed a soda from her fridge and decided to catch up on a little office work on her computer. She smiled. Once Evan got home, who knew when she'd be interested in checking emails again? She'd have better things to do.

She checked her own personal stuff first. Not much there. Then she decided to go ahead and check Lisa Sinclair's emails. She knew there would be new ones. Undoubtedly Morel had sent her some since she'd turned off the email indicator chirps on her phone.

And there were. Juliet was aghast to see fifty-seven new messages in the past two days.

Oh my God. Morel was obviously more sick than they had thought. Being around Juliet and seeing her on the yacht must have made him downright crazy.

Fifty-seven messages.

At one time she would have read them all. Pored over each one, here alone, fighting and losing the battle to not let fear overwhelm her.

But she wasn't going to do that. Not tonight. She'd wait until tomorrow, or the day after, when Evan, or even the entire Omega staff, was with her. Waiting didn't make her weak or a coward. It meant she was growing, learning. Facing her fears in a better, more effective, way.

She would just go on over to Evan's house. She didn't need to stay here anymore. But as she scrolled up to close the email account, she noticed the date and time of the latest sweetheart email that had been sent.

Today. Five minutes ago.

What the hell? This one Juliet opened.

Just you and me together at last, sweetheart. We've had to wait a long time, haven't we? You're so beautiful.

She sat staring at the screen. If Heath Morel was in custody, there was no way he could've sent that email.

And then she smelled it, a sickly sweet odor coming from her hallway. One she recognized from just a few days before. The smell of a cigar.

Oh no, they'd made a horrible mistake. Juliet turned slowly in her chair and faced the doorway.

There stood Christopher Cady. "Hello, my sweetheart."

EVAN WATCHED FROM the other side of the two-way mirror as Cameron and Sawyer questioned Morel. Dylan watched with him, since he wasn't actually law enforcement.

For nearly forty-five minutes Cameron and Sawyer had been at it, at first drilling Morel about his criminal activities, although very specifically not mentioning Vince Cady, and then moving on to the emails sent to Lisa Sinclair. Morel had looked a little uncomfortable when they'd mentioned his shady activities, although he hadn't said anything that incriminated himself. But his stare was completely blank when they mentioned the emails.

"I know I've been out of the game for a few years," Dylan said to Evan as they both watched the action in the interrogation room. "But if I had to guess, I would say that Morel has no idea what they're talking about with the emails."

"But I've read them all, Dylan. They contain details that no one could know if they hadn't been there or been communicating with Robert Avilo. And Avilo hasn't been communicating with anyone. It has to be Morel."

Through the glass, Cameron continued questioning the man, but Sawyer was looking at a text he'd just received. Confusion suffused his face and he glanced over at the two-way mirror. When he walked over to Cameron and showed him the text, his brother got the same befuddled look, then gestured with his head for Sawyer to go to the observation room.

"What's going on?" Evan demanded as soon as he arrived.

"I just got a text from Megan. She's still at the Omega computer lab. She said another email came in for Lisa Sinclair fifteen minutes ago."

"Is it on a scheduled timer or something?" Dylan asked.

"No. It was actually sent then. No timer. Megan is sure."

Nobody dismissed Sawyer's fiancée. She was smarter than all three of them put together.

But if she was right, that meant Heath Morel wasn't their perp. Damn it, Evan had really wanted this to be over with.

He rubbed his eyes. "Okay, I guess it's not him, then. Tell Cam to ask a few more random questions to throw Morel off any scent and—"

Evan froze as his and every other phone in the room began buzzing. They all grabbed for them. Another text from Megan at the Omega office.

Juliet had just activated the emergency transmitter in her locket. She was in trouble.

Evan was running out the door before he even finished reading the message. Dylan and Sawyer were right behind him. Cameron would have to stay with Morel.

They made it to the car, Evan letting Dylan drive because of his shoulder. Sawyer was already on the phone with Megan. He put her on speaker.

"Honey, what's going on?"

"Juliet pushed the panic button on the locket." They could all hear Megan clicking away at the keyboard while speaking to them. Multitasking wasn't a problem for her.

"Are you sure it wasn't an accident or something? A mistake?"

"No, setting it off accidentally is nearly impossible. And I've already tried to call and text her. No response."

"Is the tracker working, Megan?" Evan asked.

"Yes, Evan. She's at her house. She hasn't moved any significant distance since the transmitter was turned on."

Evan tried not to panic. There was more than one reason Juliet could have hit the emergency button without it actually being a life-threatening situation. She'd gotten smacked around by the Ukrainians pretty hard. Maybe she was just having problems from that.

Evan could recognize the holes in his own theory, but

he clung to it. He couldn't stand the thought of her being hurt again.

As if Dylan could read Evan's thoughts, he pushed down on the gas and the car shot forward.

Juliet wouldn't have activated the device if it wasn't truly an emergency. Everybody in the car knew that.

"Oh crap," Megan said. Evan had forgotten they still had her on speakerphone.

"What?" All three men responded in unison.

"Hold. Processing." Megan was a scientist to her core. If she was telling them to wait, she had a good reason to do so, but those moments were some of the longest in Evan's life.

"Oh crap," she repeated.

Evan closed his eyes and forced himself not to scream at her.

"We've been digging more deeply into Robert Avilo, since he knew the most about Juliet's rape. Details that were in the emails."

"Yeah?" Evan replied. "Juliet talked to the warden at his prison and he said Avilo hadn't had any contact—written, phone calls, visitors, anything—since he'd been in jail. Evidently Robert's brother Marco was his only friend, and Marco's dead."

Good thing, too, because Evan was pretty sure he would've killed him for what he'd done to Juliet if the man wasn't already in the ground.

"No, that looks correct. Robert Avilo hasn't had any outside contact with anyone, as far as we can tell," Megan confirmed.

"But..." Evan prodded.

"But Avilo's cellmate sends out letters all the time. Sometimes two or three a week. All going to the same person and place. His cousin, a resident of a mental hospital–country club type place in Croatia."

"Croatia? Like Europe Croatia?" Evan asked. And what the hell did this have to do with Juliet?

"It's a place where rich parents send their bad teenagers and young adults when they've gotten into trouble, and they want to keep them out of prison or out of sight. Non-extradition. Of course, that's interesting, because Croatia has traditionally been a democratic-supporting country at least in terms of socioeconomic—"

"Honey," Sawyer said. "Focus."

"I'm sorry," Megan replied. "Anyway, Robert Avilo's roommate writes to his cousin there all the time. We were able to get a scan of one of the letters, and although it doesn't mention any names, it definitely includes some details about a rape."

Evan could feel cold pooling in his chest. "Who is the cousin, Megan?"

"It's not the cousin that's a big deal. It's the cousin's BFF at the hospital, who was just released back to his family about six months ago."

"Who?"

"Christopher Cady. Vince's son. According to records I hacked, Cady sent him there five years ago at the ripe old age of seventeen, after a fourth woman claimed Christopher attacked her. The Cady family couldn't buy her off, like they had the others, so needed him out of the country quick."

"Juliet said the emails have been coming for about a year," Evan stated. "Would Christopher have had access to email at this hospital place?"

"Without a doubt. It's not a prison, it's more of a retreat. And when Cady got home six months ago? That's when the pickup in emails really started."

So many things made sense. How the emails became more excitable a few days ago, after Cady met Juliet for the first time. And the looks Evan had seen on Christopher's face while on the yacht.

Obsession.

A man obsessed with Juliet had her in his clutches. The cold in Evan's chest spread further.

"Wait, she's on the move now, actually headed toward you." Megan provided them coordinates. "Do you want me to send in local PD?"

"No," Evan told her. "Police might cause Christopher to do something desperate. But have them on standby." Evan didn't want to risk Juliet's life.

"Hurry," Megan said. "If she gets out of range, we'll lose her. That transmitter is limited. I'll keep giving you coordinates. Right now, she's still headed north."

"Drive faster," Evan whispered to Dylan. He prayed they would get to her in time.

Chapter Twenty-Five

Christopher Cady was certifiably insane. Juliet wasn't sure how she hadn't seen it before. Now she wished when she'd flipped him on the yacht that he'd fallen overboard.

Because he was crazy. He really was.

He had found her by tracking her phone, Christopher had told her. They were in his car back at Annapolis Harbor. Juliet had driven, with Christopher pointing his gun at her and stroking her hair the entire way.

The gun didn't freak her out nearly as much as the hair-stroking did. Every touch caused her to cringe, flinch, her flesh crawling.

She had to keep it together, keep her wits about her, and pray like never before that the emergency transmitter in her necklace was working.

Evan would get to her. He had to.

She couldn't believe they were back at Annapolis Harbor. From where they were parked, Juliet could see the unique three-pronged flagpole in the middle of Susan Campbell Park. It was late; the harbor was empty. Juliet had tried to buy more time by driving as slowly as possible, but she could go only so slow without Christopher realizing she was stalling.

"I know you don't love me now, sweetheart." Christopher twisted a strand of her hair between his fingers as they sat in the parked car. “But you will. I have another boat, one that doesn’t require a staff. It will be just you and me.”

He got out of the car, keeping his gun pointed at her the entire time as he walked around to her door. He opened it and pulled her out.

“Christopher, what about Bob? I’m married. I can’t just leave him and run off with you.”

“Don’t worry. I’m going to get you situated in the boat, then come back and finish your husband for good.”

“What?”

“He doesn’t deserve to live, sweetheart. He didn’t protect you when you needed it most. Not eighteen months ago and not yesterday.”

“Christopher—” Juliet wanted to break through to her captor, but there didn’t seem to be much chance.

“It was *me* who protected you yesterday, not him. Because we are meant to be together, you and I.”

Juliet wasn’t prepared for Christopher’s kiss. Something snapped in her. She bit down on his lip and then pushed him away with all her strength.

But he was ready for that. She found herself being spun around and flung against the car, Christopher using his weight to hold her there while he yanked her arms behind her back and bound her wrists together with a zip tie. Juliet tried to breathe through the panic.

“I should be angry, but I’m not. You’re not ready yet, but you will be soon.” He tightened the tie. “This will just help me keep you on the boat until I can take care of Bob. I have to admit I was hoping he would be with you at your house, so I could get rid of him before even talking to you.”

Thank God they’d arrested Heath Morel and Evan had gone with her brothers to question him. Otherwise, Evan would probably be dead now.

Christopher grabbed Juliet by the arm and started marching her toward the pier. She knew she couldn't allow him to get her on that boat. If she did it would cost both her and Evan their lives.

"Stay quiet. If you yell and someone comes to investigate, I'll be forced to kill them. You don't want that on your conscience, do you?"

No, she didn't, but she didn't want to get on that vessel with this lunatic, either. The docks were pretty quiet at this time of night and Juliet didn't see anyone she could yell to, anyway.

They were nearing the boat slips now, Christopher angling her toward one of the last ones, where a large sailboat floated serenely in the water. Under other circumstances Juliet would have loved to climb aboard, but now she just wanted to get away. She kept testing the zip tie, hoping to find a way out of it, but to no avail.

She would have to try to fight Christopher with her arms restrained. Because she sure as hell wasn't getting on the boat of her own accord.

Juliet tensed, about to make a move by throwing herself back at Christopher, when a voice called out from the darkness. "I'm not going to let you just take my wife, Christopher."

Evan. Thank God.

Christopher immediately turned toward him, using Juliet as a shield. The two men pointed their weapons at each other.

"You don't deserve her. You don't take care of her. Don't protect her. She deserves to be with me." Christopher spat the words.

"Well..." Evan took a step forward, weapon still raised. "Why don't we go sit down and talk about this, the three of us? If Lisa wants to leave me to be with you, I'm man enough to accept that."

"No!" Christopher's near hysteria echoed now. "You would try to trick her."

He took another few steps backward, dragging Juliet with him until they were on the gangplank that led to the boat.

"Just put the gun down, Christopher, before someone gets hurt." Evan tried to talk reason into the younger man, but he was far beyond that at this point.

"You're the only one who's going to get hurt!" he growled.

Juliet realized he was no longer waving his gun so wildly. He was taking aim at Evan, ready to shoot.

"No!" She screamed, throwing her weight into her captor, but he had already gotten off a shot.

Christopher crumpled onto her. He had been shot from a different angle, not by Evan. He seemed to be badly wounded, but wasn't dead. His eyes fastened on hers as they hit the railing of the gangplank together.

"It's over, Christopher. Bob's never going to let you leave here with me. Just let me go," she told the younger man.

Christopher looked over toward Evan, then back at her. He ran his fingers, now bloody, down her cheek. "We're destined to be together, sweetheart. Even if it's in death."

Before Juliet could figure out what he meant to do, he threw all his weight forward over the railing, dragging her with him. She could hear Evan yelling for her as she fell with a splash into Annapolis Harbor.

The freezing water stole Juliet's breath. Darkness and cold surrounded her, making orientation impossible. She fought to free herself from Christopher's grip, but with her arms tied behind her back, there was little she could do. He didn't fight, just wrapped his arms around her as they sank deeper and deeper. She finally hit the bottom of the harbor, landing face-first, with him on top of her.

Juliet's lungs screamed for air. She bucked and twisted, to no avail, and was giving up hope when she felt Christopher's body finally—*finally*—shift away. In the dark water she couldn't tell what had happened. Had he lost consciousness? Died? Had someone pulled him off?

Juliet pushed off against the bottom as hard as she could, then kept kicking, but it wasn't enough. With her hands restrained behind her back and the weight of her waterlogged clothes and shoes, she couldn't get to the surface. She fought as hard as she could, but couldn't reach the precious air. Juliet wasn't even sure if she was heading in the right direction any longer. Blackness surrounded her.

She wouldn't give up. She kept kicking, but the need for oxygen overrode everything. Instinct took over and she opened her mouth to breathe, but all she took in was water.

She stopped fighting as the blackness consumed her.

EVAN DIVED UNDER the water of the harbor again, as did Dylan and Sawyer. All of them screaming for Juliet.

It had been only moments since Christopher Cady had pulled her into the dark bay. But they were running out of time. *Juliet* was running out of time. Evan had found Cady in the depths, but hadn't been able to find her. Evan didn't even bother dragging Christopher up, just pushed him aside and kept searching for Juliet.

He couldn't lose her. Not now, when they'd really just found each other.

But the black water seemed to swallow everything whole.

Evan wouldn't give up. No matter what, he would keep searching for Juliet. He dived again, but in the opposite direction from where they'd been searching. He stretched his arms out as far as they would reach, hoping to feel her, since there was no way he'd be able to see her. He swam around until the need for air once again forced him upward.

And that's when he felt something hit against his ankle. He immediately spun around in the water.

Juliet!

But she wasn't swimming. Oh God, she wasn't moving at all.

Evan grabbed her lifeless form and began dragging them both toward the surface. As he broke through, drawing in much-needed air, he realized Juliet wasn't breathing.

"Sawyer, Dylan! I've got her!" They had to get her to shore so they could start CPR. It wasn't too late. She hadn't been in there that long.

It couldn't be too late.

Evan dragged Juliet over to the pier, where her brothers had made their way out of the water. He handed her still form up to them.

Somebody cut the zip tie off her hands so she could lie flat on the pier. Both her brothers immediately began CPR, one giving breaths, one doing chest compressions, as Evan climbed up beside them.

In the pale light of the poorly lit pier, Juliet's skin had a horrible bluish tinge to it. He didn't know if it was from cold or lack of oxygen. Her lifelessness was the scariest thing Evan had ever seen.

He knelt beside her. "Come on, baby. Don't you give up. Not now, not when we've just found each other." Evan didn't care if her brothers heard.

"Jules, I love you. I always have. Fight, baby. Fight for us." Evan couldn't stop the tears that were streaming down his cheeks. "I love you. I can't live without you," he whispered.

Juliet's whole body seemed to convulse, causing her brothers to stop the CPR and pull back. They turned her to the side as she vomited half the harbor. Finally, she rolled onto her back of her own accord. Although she shivered, her skin had lost much of its blue tinge. Dylan and Sawyer slid her over and began wrapping their dry jackets, which they'd left on the dock before diving into the water to save Juliet, around her for warmth.

Juliet had eyes only for Evan. "Hey." Her voice was raspy, strained from the vomiting.

Evan smiled and pushed a strand of hair out of her face. "Hey, gorgeous."

Sawyer slapped him on the back. "Congrats, man. First time I've seen a declaration of undying love cause a woman to puke her guts out. Impressive."

Evan smiled, but didn't take his eyes from Juliet.

"You want to tell me exactly what's going on with you two?" Sawyer asked.

"We'll give you guys a minute." Dylan cut Sawyer off. "Go call this in. Get Jules a real blanket." He grabbed his younger brother and start pulling him away, despite Sawyer's indignant responses.

All Evan wanted to do was look at Juliet. To touch her. To know she was alive.

"I heard you, you know," she croaked. "So did my brothers. No going back now, because I love you, too. You're stuck with me."

Relief flooded Evan, chasing away every last bit of panic. Juliet loved him the way he loved her.

"I wouldn't have it any other way." He took her hand in his. "You're still wearing Lisa Sinclair's wedding band, you know."

"Yeah, I didn't have a chance to take it off."

"How about if we get a set that's yours and mine, rather than Lisa and Bob's?"

Juliet smiled even though she was shivering. "You've got yourself a deal. Although I'm going to make you propose again, properly this time, once you get me a ring."

She started to sit up, so Evan helped her. "That would be my pleasure." He wrapped his arms around her and pulled her close.

"But we'll still get to be Lisa and Bob in the future, right? I want to take Vince Cady down," Juliet told him from against his chest. A worried note came into her voice. "Do you think we've ruined everything with the case? Christopher's dead, right?"

"Don't worry. You and I won't even be placed at the scene by the time the report gets back to Vince Cady. Bob and Lisa will have their chance to make sure Cady goes down."

"Good. I'm ready, not so scared anymore."

Evan kissed her forehead. "There will be times when we're both scared, but we'll face it together. You and I make a pretty good team."

"Both on cases and off." She pulled his arms more securely around her.

Neither of them had any doubts about it.

* * * * *

Janie Crouch's OMEGA SECTOR *miniseries comes to a gripping conclusion next month with Dylan's story. Look for LEVERAGE wherever Harlequin Intrigue books and ebooks are sold!*

SPECIAL EXCERPT FROM

HARLEQUIN

INTRIGUE

Navy SEAL "Rip" Cord Schafer's mission is not a one-man operation, but never in his wildest dreams did he imagine teaming up with a woman: Covert Cowboy operative Tracie Kosart.

Read on for a sneak peek at
NAVY SEAL NEWLYWED,
the newest installment from
Elle James's
COVERT COWBOYS, INC.

"How do I know you really work for Hank?"

"You don't. But has anyone else shown up and told you he's your contact?" She raised her eyebrows, the saucy expression doing funny things to his insides. "So, do you trust me, or not?"

His lips curled upward on the ends. "I'll go with not."

"Oh, come on, sweetheart." She batted her pretty green eyes and gave him a sexy smile. "What's not to trust?"

His gaze scraped over her form. "I expected a cowboy, not a…"

"Cow*girl*?" Her smile sank and she slipped into the driver's seat. Her lips firmed into a straight line. "Are you coming or not? If you're dead set on a cowboy, I'll contact Hank and tell him to send a male replacement. But then he'd have to come up with another plan."

"I'm interested in how you and Hank plan to help. Frankly, I'd rather my SEAL team had my six."

"Yeah, but you're deceased. Using your SEAL team would only alert your assassin that you aren't as dead as the navy claims you are. How long do you think you'll last once that bit of news leaks out?"

His lips pressed together. "I'd survive."

"By going undercover? Then you still won't have the backing of your team, and we're back to the original plan." She grinned. "Me."

Rip sighed. "Fine. I want to head back to Honduras and trace the weapons back to where they're coming from. What's Hank's plan?"

"For me to work with you." She pulled a large envelope from between her seat and the console and handed it across to him. "Everything we need is in that packet."

Rip riffled through the contents of the packet, glancing at a passport with his picture on it as well as a name he'd never seen. "Chuck Gideon?"

"Better get used to it."

"Speaking of names...we've already kissed and you haven't told me who you are." Rip glanced her way briefly. "Is it a secret? Do you have a shady past or are you related to someone important?"

"For this mission, I'm related to someone important." She twisted her lips and sent a crooked grin his way. "You. For the purpose of this operation, you can call me Phyllis. Phyllis Gideon. I'll be your wife."

Love the Harlequin book you just read?

Your opinion matters.

Review this book on your favorite book site, review site, blog or your own social media properties and share your opinion with other readers!

Be sure to connect with us at:
Harlequin.com/Newsletters
Facebook.com/HarlequinBooks
Twitter.com/HarlequinBooks